PRETTY KITTEN

AGE OF NIGHT BOOK TWO

MAY SAGE

To Andie,

Lovely meeting you ♡

MaySage

PERKS

*D*aunte stormed into the pride house, hoping to catch his Alphas before they left for their appointment; souring his humor wasn't an easy feat, but the events of the morning had managed that, and then some. He needed to speak to Rygan and Aisling. Maybe they'd say he'd made the wrong decision. It wasn't too late to get back to the bus station and help the poor girl he'd all but abandoned there.

The large, modern home was bathed in sunlight, courtesy of the front wall, all made of reflective glass. Inside, under the watchful eye of a couple of domestic cats, half a dozen children were attempting to throttle two fully grown feline shifter Enforcers - and managing, by the looks of it. Tracy and Coveney were doing their best to keep them at bay, and failing miserably.

His foul mood evaporated, as if sucked right out of his lungs, and, at the same time, his resolution faded. Yes, if he appealed to them, his Alphas would tell him he could go find the girl he wished to help, and offer her their protection. But in doing so, he would endanger this. All those children playing, the peaceful family they'd earned out of sweat and blood.

He couldn't do that. He'd speak to Rye later. He'd tell him what had happened - but he would also say that the girl was long gone, beyond their reach. It wasn't being selfish; it was being a Beta. Putting the wellbeing of his pride first.

Alphas were cut to give orders and protect those in need - that could extend to mere strangers. Betas did the dirty work. *This* was what his position required. Making sacrifices, and living with the guilt if he had to.

"Where's Hsu?" he asked, counting only seven kids in the lounge.

Niamh, Jasper, Clive, Victoria, Will, Daniel, and even little Lola were ganging up against the Enforcers - the toddler sat on the floor, holding on to one of Coveney's legs. But there was no sign of the last child.

It wasn't a rare occurrence; Hsu liked her own company. She wasn't pushed away by the other kids, and they didn't take her need to be alone to heart, either. She was a Seer, which meant she had visions practically every day - time stopped around her as she stared in the emptiness. No wonder she didn't feel comfortable doing so around everyone else.

"She was having a nap," Will offered, all the while tickling Tracy's knee.

Dirty trick. "She has to wake up soon, though. As soon as we win, Tracy and Coveney have to take us out to an amusement park!"

So, that was what the battle of the day had been about.

"I'll go get her," he offered, shaking his head in amusement.

Those kids would willingly go against an entire army if that meant a day out of Lakesides; and Daunte couldn't exactly blame them. Their small town was everything they needed; simple, quiet- but, in truth, for children of their ages, that meant *boring*.

He walked back to the entryway from the living room, ready to climb up to the second floor to get to the children's room, but Hsu sat on the first step of the curved staircase, her little head of curls resting against the bannister.

"There!" Daunte said, fingers pointed right at her. "There's the perfect representation of *doom and gloom*. I'm pretty sure if I googled it, I'd find a picture of you just like that."

The kid cracked a smile as he sat down next to her.

That was another part of his job; taking care of the morale of the pride, and that included the children, as well as the adults. He would have taken the time to check up on any of them.

That was doubly true for Hsu. None of the children knew, of course, and the pride had every intention of keeping it that way because it shouldn't matter, but, legally speaking, they'd had to adopt the children on a one on one basis. There was a piece of paper somewhere in Rye's office saying that Hsu was *his* daughter. And really, it *didn't* matter. He took care of all the kids; they all did. But everything in him made him want to claw out of his skin when she made that sad face.

They'd never discussed it, but he could see that Coveney was as protective of Victoria, Tracy of Will, Ian of Daniel and Clive, Ola of Jasper, and Rye, of Niamh and Lola. Their kids. Funny how a dusty document had a hold on them.

"What's up, little one?" he asked her and, for a beat, she kept her mouth shut.

Eventually, she asked, "If you knew something was going to happen, do you have to say it?"

That made him pause. Hsu had always shared her visions; this was the very first time he'd heard her having any doubt about whether she should.

"It depends, poppet. Why do you ask?"

Her little face scrunched up in an adorable moue.

"Some people won't be happy. They might try to stop

it. But I think it's good. I don't want my vision to be stopped."

Oh, goodie; a philosophical question before it was time for brandy. After the morning he'd had, Daunte was already close to having a headache, and now this.

He played and replied half a dozen responses in his head, taking his time, as Hsu looked up to him like what he was about to say should be engraved on holy stone tablets.

Kids. Why, oh, why did they always expect adults to have their shit together?

"Hsu Wyvern, there's something you need to know- and not doubt for a second. Ever. You're not our Seer. You're not obliged by some oath to share *any* vision with us. The pride house could burn to the ground tomorrow and you wouldn't *have* to warn us. You're our child. We'll love you regardless of what you see - and regardless of what you tell us. Understood?"

She looked up at him with stars in her eyes, before launching herself at him and wrapping her little arms around his neck.

Yeah. Sometimes, being Beta wasn't such a bad thing.

DROOL-WORTHY ARCHENEMY

*S*ome guys shouldn't be allowed to wear shirts. For the greater good. Seriously, men like him walking around half naked could genuinely cause worldwide peace. Women would be too busy melting into puddles of lust to get up to any evildoings, and men would just spend their days and nights doing pushups in hopes of eventually looking like him.

Daunte Cross. Otherwise known as Clari's nemesis; well, when he wasn't half naked.

"You're drooling."

Highly possible. Also, no one - absolutely no one in the entire universe - could blame her right now. Daunte was washing his jeep with a sponge and a bucket of water. Apparently, that had required removing his shirt and getting the top half of his sculpted body wet and glistening in the sunlight.

She approved. Whole-heartedly.

"And you're not? What's wrong with you!" she asked the small, pretty, and very pregnant brunette standing next to her.

Ace - Aisling Cross-Wayland - had come to meet her at the door, as she always did, because she liked to have first pick of the leftovers Clari brought back from the bakery. She pushed to her tiptoes, one hand on her extended belly, and peeked into the box of goodies in Clari's hands, before grabbing a cupcake.

"Because," she replied, licking her fingers clean of frosting, "he happens to be my baby brother, so he's gross."

Gross. Clari tilted her head and concentrated, trying to determine what could potentially be considered "gross" about the tanned Adonis.

Then he turned and his eyes narrowed when he found her on the doorstep. She remembered. The man was a first-class jerk to her.

"Yep," she nodded emphatically. "Totally gross."

Clari shouldn't have cared but she had never - not even once - directly interacted with him. She didn't speak to him, they didn't even say hello to each other. He was just included in a queenly wave she awkwardly executed whenever she met the members of the

Wyvern pride of feline shifters. So, every day. Literally, every day. She worked for Aisling, their Alpha female, and she didn't have a life. Taking some time off meant watching too many B movies and inhaling her weight in popcorn from her sofa, so she avoided doing it as much as possible.

She got along with every member of the pride, even those who generally communicated by grunts, like Coveney. Everyone except Daunte. He'd been an ass from day one, glaring like her very existence was an insult to him.

She knew that there was a fair bit of racism on both sides of the spectrum - humans who hated shifters on sight and shifters who couldn't stand humans – and, at first, she'd believed that had been the problem, but she'd since seen Daunte interact with other humans in Lakesides. He smiled at them. Like, really smiled, without baring his teeth like he was about to take a bite.

That's when she'd taken to imagining his annoyingly handsome face on the target when she threw darts at the pub. She never missed the bull's eye now. Whatever his problem was with her, it was personal, which annoyed her. She hadn't done anything to him, dammit.

"How was work?" Aisling asked, with a certain degree of indifference.

A few months back, she'd done everything in the

bakery, baking, selling, accounting, while Clari had just delivered the goodies. Things had changed when the Wyvern Pride had turned up; she'd taken a step back and Clari had started taking on more responsibilities.

Ace still popped by almost every day, to bake, to supervise their two new employees, and do little things here and there, but the bakery had become Clari's thing, too. She'd almost felt guilty at finding an undue amount of pride and concern for a business that wasn't really hers, until recently. Last week, Ace had presented her with a pretty document printed on thick paper, and told her it needed her signature. She'd made her a partner. Clari still couldn't wrap her mind around it. Sure, it wasn't, and wouldn't ever be, a multi-million dollar corporation, but she had a business now. The thought still made her teary.

"Exhausting. We totally need another pair of hands on Saturdays."

They both knew that, but they lived in a small town seemingly inhabited by children and their grandparents; there weren't a lot of potential part-time employees. Clari had cooked up an idea weeks ago, but she hadn't voiced it, feeling like she might be stepping on someone's toes. Biting her lip, she spelled it out, "But, hey, I was just wondering if Niamh would want to do a few hours a week. You know, like a summer job. Get some work experience, or something."

Yep, she was rambling.

Niamh was one of the children the Pride had adopted into their fold; she'd just turned thirteen, and, from a vantage point of view, Clari saw just how bored and frustrated she was, stuck in the middle of nowhere, without meeting anyone her age. She expressed her annoyance by buying tight, revealing clothing and rolling her eyes at the first provocation, knowing full well that it made the adults want to strangle her pretty neck.

Clari felt uncomfortable in her shoes as Ace's amber eyes focused on her, unblinking. She didn't often see it, but right now, it was obvious that she was dealing with Aisling, the Alpha that could dismember a man twice her size with one hand tied behind her back.

"Hm," was all she said, before calling out, "Rye!"

Oh, shit.

Clari froze. She didn't fear Rygan Wayland, not *exactly*, but he was a dominant, powerful Alpha, and, unlike his mate, he wasn't her personal friend. Why did Ace want him here?

She forced herself to breath in and out. Of course she called him. This was a pride decision; she wasn't going to jump in without speaking with her partner first.

Ace laughed a little.

"You know, for a human, you're very attuned to the dynamic of prides. You always act like a shifter when you see Rye."

"A submissive shifter, you mean," she grumbled, annoyed by her own reactions.

It wasn't like Rye was going to do anything to her. Hell, she was pretty sure that the man would actually protect her if she ever needed him to. Jas and Ian liked to call her an honorary member of the pride. Mostly because they loved cake.

Ace shook her head.

"No, I don't think so. Submissives are normally appeased by high levels of dominance because shifters don't tend to attack them. Well, sane shifters, anyway. You act like a dominant who doesn't want to be forced into submission. Me," she said, pointing to herself, "you defer to. But the others; Jas, Ola, Ian, Coveney-you try to push when you can. It's just Rye who makes you squirm because you know he tops you and it's bugging you."

Clari lifted a brow, intrigued, and flattered. She hated the idea of submission, so it was comforting to know that Ace didn't think it was in her nature. Not that it mattered. She was human, so, whatever.

"No comment on the fact that I didn't mention Daunte?" Ace teased her.

Although she hadn't actually spelled it out, her friend had caught on early about her unrequited admiration for the dick who treated her like trash.

"I'll tell you what I think, regardless. You're going

around in a circle, ready to pounce. Someday, one of you will take the first step and determine who comes out on top."

Clari opened her mouth and closed it a few times in a row, not finding her words. Finally, all she could say was, "Whatever."

STATUS QUO

*R*ye made it downstairs right then, a phone in hand, smoothly speaking about the stock exchange or something equally boring. His cold blue eyes twinkled as he took in his mate, and a lazy smile settled on his lips. He bent to touch her extended tummy with one hand, and pressed his lips on her shoulder. Clari felt almost voyeuristic, but couldn't avert her eyes because that was so damn cute she wanted to bottle it.

"Coffee?" she mouthed, desperate for something to do.

The Alpha male smiled at her gratefully, acquiescing, and Ace glared. Coffee was one of the many life necessities she'd had to forgo for the good of her unborn baby.

"Decaf vanilla latte," Ace growled, visibly resenting each word.

Clari walked out of the entryway and into the open-plan living room, where most of the pride members normally gathered in their down time. Right now, there was only Ian on the sofa, which meant Coveney was probably patrolling, and, as the rest of house seemed quiet, someone had taken the kids out - Ola, or Jas.

"Hey, Ian. Coffee?"

"Please."

Their kitchen had the very latest tech, producing the very best drinks in town. Which, come to think of it, may be another reason why she was here so damn often.

Rubbing her hands together like the average cartoon villain, she got the coffeemaker started and prepared four cups.

"Hello, Beastie," she greeted the lynx who'd strolled in the kitchen area and come to rub against her leg.

Beastie didn't acknowledge the presence of any of the shifters except Ace, but he tolerated Niamh and Clari when he wanted food or a scratch. She got a pouch of wet food out and served His Furry Highness at her feet. The animal consented to eat without clawing her tights first, this time.

Beastie and their coffeemaker were just a couple of

the many things that make Clari love hanging out at the pride house.

"You still need to explain why your coffee is so much better than when anyone else makes it," Ian called from the living room.

And there was also that; the fact that *most of them* liked to make her feel welcome.

"Secret," she lied.

Her reason wasn't exactly glamorous. She'd worked as a barista during her four years away at college; her family had always been very generous with their wallets, but Clari hated asking for money. It had helped pay for anything extracurricular, like her impressive collection of shoes currently collecting dust in her cupboard. Lakesides wasn't exactly the sort of place where one wore Louboutin.

In all honesty, she wasn't one hundred percent sure why she'd come back to her home town. Or rather, she'd known why she'd come back – but it had been meant to be a quick visit. The reason why she stayed was a mystery, though. She'd left as quickly as she could, and she'd loved it in the city, but here she was. She'd told herself it was temporary at first – a break until she knew where she wanted to land for good, but that became more of a lie every day. She felt comfortable here.

And it might have something to do with the pride of

young feline shifters who made it feel like a fun version of home.

"Where's everyone?"

"Water park. The lucky buggers managed to rope Tracy, Coveney, and Christine into taking them, so Ace and Rye said they could go."

Ian sounded grumpy, and she guessed it was because he'd been left behind; unlike their domestic counterparts, most big cats loved water, and, well, anyone living in Lakesides in the summer could appreciate the benefits of an afternoon playing in a pool.

"Well, more Bakewell tart for you, then."

That seemed to cheer him up; he got up, looked in the box she carried, and gave her a goofy smile as he piled three pieces in one of his hands.

"You're a beautiful creature, Clarissa," he told her, pointing right to her face, before stuffing a tart in his mouth.

Men and their stomachs.

She was rolling her eyes when she caught something at the corner of her eye, and stiffened.

Daunte had put a shirt back on, although his hair was still wet and waving a little, like Superman's. He stood close to the door and glared like it was going out of fashion.

Any other day, she would just have pretended to

ignore him, or glared right back, but something Ace had said made her want to push him. Cats circling each other, waiting to pounce? That seemed accurate enough. And she had every intention of being the one on top.

"Coffee?"

HELL OF A DAY

*S*he was talking to him. Why was she talking to him? It wasn't how their dynamic worked.

Shit, he loved her voice. "Coffee," that's all she'd said, and he was hard. She was looking directly at him, her emerald green eyes blazing defiantly. She knew what she'd done. She knew she'd broken the status quo.

Why? Why today? As though Daunte didn't have enough on his mind already. Clarissa Thompson didn't have to do anything to mess with his brain; the fact that she existed already achieved that. He thought of her every day since he'd first seen her, inhaled her scent, heard that damn voice.

And now, she asked him if he wanted coffee. Made by her. He grunted something that he hoped resembled a yes, while Ian attempted to hide his shit-eating grin behind a newspaper. Daunte flipped him off as soon as Clari turned her back.

"Done with your truck?"

Again. She was doing it again. The talking thing.

"Yep. All spotless."

"One might wonder why you cleaned it again; didn't you get it done just last week?"

Daunte shot Ian a cautioning look; he could understand why the man would tease him about his awkwardness in front of Clari - he could have a look in the mirror and see just how fucking laughable he was. If it had been another guy, he would have been just as ready to take the piss - but this was different. The problem with his truck was a serious issue that concerned the pride's safety, and he hadn't even had the chance to speak to Rye about it.

Ian immediately dropped it, catching on to the difference in his expression; Daunte didn't take most things too seriously. The one and only notable exception was pride business.

There wasn't anything *too* obvious about him being overzealous with his truck, but the problem was that they were cats - by nature, they wanted to know every single little detail. If the wrong person heard that, and caught his reluctance when he replied, he was screwed.

Ace and Rye walked in, and immediately the

atmosphere of the room changed; everyone involuntarily straightened up a little. Their Alphas didn't demand that sort of deference, but they naturally commanded it.

The couple had spent the afternoon with their midwife; they'd religiously attended training meetings that were supposed to somehow help when his sister was going to push the balloon she was carrying around out of her teeny, tiny body. Daunte winced every time he thought about it. Now that she was only a few days away from giving birth, he felt positively sick. He'd never do that to a woman.

"How's everything?" he asked Ace. She opened her mouth, but he held his hands up. "That was mostly rhetorical. You're just meant to say, you're good."

The damn woman took a vicious pleasure in giving him details when he didn't stop her. He'd thrown up as much as she had during her first trimester.

"We're great," Rye replied, sparing him. "They say we're good to go in about ten days now."

He was smiling from ear to ear.

Then his intense gaze looked around, and fell on the most vulnerable thing in the room.

A tray in hand, Clarissa came out of the kitchen area, and walked right to them; he didn't think anyone had given her a Shifter 101, yet she always did the right thing. She went to serve the Alphas first.

"Ace told me you thought of asking Niamh to work at the bakery this summer?"

Clari nodded enthusiastically.

"Yep. I could train her on weekdays when we're quiet, and she could help on weekends. She's a bright kid, I'm sure she'll make herself useful. Plus, it would be a change of scenery, you know?"

"What?" Daunte growled, completely baffled.

That was the worst idea of the century. Niamh was a witch - a teenage witch, just discovering her powers, and with a mile-long attitude. They wanted a *human* to supervise her?

Yet, ignoring him, Rye nodded.

"It's brilliant."

"I'm actually ashamed I didn't think of it myself," Ace piped in. "Baby brain, maybe. She's bored here, and she makes us pay for it. Plus, we could pay her some money, which means she'll have her own playtime fund. I loved that at her age."

"That's the most stupid idea I ever heard of," Daunte proclaimed, but somehow, everyone ignored him. Again.

"She might be a little too young to be on the books legally," Clari admitted, and Ace shook her head.

"Shifter laws are a little different. We're expected to raise our kids to take their place in the pride when they're ready. I can write her in; it means applying for a license but it's a simple formality."

He couldn't believe his ears. Daunte took a step forward, placing himself between the Alphas and Clari, arms crossed.

"That's a no. Ace, you'll be in the shop even less when the baby gets here. That means you're asking a *human* to take care of one of us. A powerful, young, volatile, one of us." Without turning, he could feel anger radiating from Clari, and he ignored it, concentrating on his Alphas. "What if Niamh hurts herself and gets upset?"

He didn't need to spell it out after that. Rye and Ace exchanged a glance, knowing exactly what he referred to. Niamh fought the other kids, learning to defend herself, and she'd twisted her ankle on a one on one with Jasper a few months back. She really hadn't meant it, and she'd stopped herself immediately, but they'd all been shocked by the strength of the wave that had followed. The humans in town had written it off as a weird natural phenomenon, an earthquake, but they knew better.

"You're right," Ace sighed.

"What?"

"Damn, it's hard to remember Clari isn't really one of us," Rye conceded.

"What?"

Daunte had every intention to carry on ignoring her, but Clari shoved his shoulders to walk past him, planting herself on the other side of him to face the Alphas.

"What is that all about? You think I'm so irresponsible I can't take care of a damn kid? And you're *listening* to him?" she sounded furious.

It probably didn't help that Daunte was smirking. He knew he'd won. The Alphas would put her safety before anything else.

"Of course not," Ace dismissed the notion with a wave of her hand. "But Daunte is right, there's more to Niamh than meets the eye. And, frankly, she needs to be around someone who can knock her out if needs be. That's why we'll have to homeschool her until she gets it under control; or we'll have to send her to a sup academy. It's really not about you. Teenage sups and humans don't mix."

Clari appeared to be slightly mollified. Daunte was practically certain the matter would have been dropped, if Ian, who generally kept to himself, hadn't piped in, "We could always set a bodyguard outside of the store when Niamh is working. I don't mind doing it. And if she makes it without incident this summer, maybe she can even try a semester at the local high school."

Daunte opened his mouth and closed it again, because there were no words to express his displeasure.

Instead, he turned his gaze on Ian, and locked it threateningly, promising reprisal. Next time they had training together, the tiger shifter was going to pay for that.

Daunte faced a conundrum. Like his father, he had no inclination towards the role of Alpha, but his level of dominance meant that he didn't like to be told what to do, and he hated when things didn't go his way. To put it simply, he was controlling as fuck. Thankfully, it generally wasn't a problem in this pride; Rye was a great Alpha, and their opinions practically never clashed.

Recently, they had - more over the last three seasons than over the last decade. And every single time, it was somehow related to Clarissa.

He wasn't stupid. He knew exactly what was happening. He'd seen it with his own eyes more than once; he'd seen it just a few months back when Rye had met his sister. He liked the girl. More worryingly, his animal was interested in her. Women didn't have to be their fated mate to hold their cat's attention.

If she'd been one of them, he would have done something about it, but she was human, so Daunte ignored it. He ignored her. Which, by the way, wasn't easy, given the fact that the woman making his animal attempt to claw his way out was at their pride house every day. Every. Single. Day. He could literally not catch a break.

Needing to think about something else - anything else, he turned to Rye and told him, "We need to talk, by the way."

Of course, that got Ace's attention; she took her mate's forearm and looked at him expectantly, visibly ready to face a hoard of dragons, if necessary. As their Alpha female, she had every right to be included in any conversation - especially the serious ones that started with *we need to talk*.

But, knowing full well that if she ever found out, she'd kick his ass for it, he did what he had to do; he lied.

"It's not pride business. Just something about a potential investment."

As he expected her to, Ace immediately rolled her eyes and walked to the sofas, disinterested.

He'd played his cards well. Now, he just needed to make sure she never heard that he had hidden something from her. Ever.

LITTLE WHITE LIES

*D*aunte Cross wasn't often ashamed, but as he explained to his Alpha what had occurred in the morning, he couldn't help but feel that he'd been an ass. He'd been on his way to look at woods close to their territory - an extension they were considering purchasing - when he'd come across one of them, a sup, in distress.

"She came out of nowhere; I almost hit her with the Jeep. When I looked at her, she was wet, dirty, sweaty, and terrified," he said, pacing around Rye's office. "She said she was kidnapped, but didn't want to go to the cops. I picked her up and got the hell out of there. As soon as she got into the Jeep, I smelled wolf on her."

"And where is she?" Rye growled, tense.

"Safe, I think. Hopefully."

He'd helped, he knew he had; but he hadn't done as much as he could have. He might have brought the girl to their territory and protected her there - they had plenty of alliances and she would have been safer. She was on the run today, by herself. But he hadn't wanted to lead problems to his pride. Simple as that. Any other time, he might have at the very least considered it, but while his sister was pregnant and vulnerable? No way, no how. Instead, he'd called Knox, the most resourceful loner he knew of, and asked him to help.

"I gave her a wad of cash - you'll see the withdrawal from the pride account, by the way - and I put her on a bus heading to LA. She'll meet Knox there. I couldn't bring her here, not with Ace ready to pop."

Unsurprisingly, his Alpha nodded curtly in understanding. He was the last person in the world who'd want to bring danger to their door days before his mate was due to give birth.

Basically, Daunte was sorry about what had happened to Emily, he empathized, sympathized, but it didn't change the fact that she wasn't part of his pride. Cold, but that was how animals survived, and shifters worked that way when they needed to. Making that sort of decision was the Beta's job.

"You did good. Knox will help her, I'm sure."

Rye's approval was anticipated, but he felt some guilt lift off his shoulders, nonetheless. Emily would be in good hands with Knox - or so he told himself. Still, Daunte wouldn't feel good about it until he knew she was safe.

"Also," Rye said uncomfortably, scratching his chin. "I guess you agree, or you wouldn't have lied to her face about the purpose of this little chat, but I really don't think you should tell Aisling about it." He visibly hated the idea of hiding anything from his mate, but, for her peace of mind, he would. "She'd freak."

She would. His sister was the strongest female he knew - hell, she topped most males - and she would hate that they didn't lend a hand to that poor girl because of her condition.

"I'm not suicidal," he replied.

If she ever found out, she was going to kick his ass into next year. And, because she was his sister, there was an unwritten rule saying that he had to let her. He'd defend himself, but he'd never attack her. Damn chivalry.

"Good. So, what about the territory you looked at?"

Daunte hesitated for a second. He hadn't spared a lot of thought to the actual goal of this morning's exploration.

"It starts on the other side of the highway and takes over most of the lake. Honestly, the forest has been burned recently, so I can't say that it's all that attractive. It'll take a lot of work to do anything lucrative with the land."

"But?"

"But," he carried on, "it's an ideal position for any enemy wishing to regroup near us."

And, unfortunately, they had an enemy who would be likely to take advantage of that, given half a chance. The pack of wolves who'd wanted to destroy them had relented, but there was no doubt that they'd try to attack again when they could.

Because of that threat, the small Wyvern Pride was currently recruiting. Rye had been reluctant at first, but they needed more members to efficiently protect their kids and survey the area. Their territory - without even counting the potential extension they'd probably purchase - was too large for ten adults to oversee.

They'd accepted applications for the last couple of months and agreed to look into potential candidates after the baby was born and Ace was back on her feet. Knowing his sister, Daunte realized that wouldn't take long.

"Also, I picked up Emily in those woods. It's obvious that whoever attacked her is using the territory for their illegal activities. It's too close to home - if something happens there, the suspicion will immediately fall on us."

That settled it in Rye's mind.

"So, we buy the land. And if they still use it afterwards, well… It's been a while since we've gone on a hunt."

Rye's eyes flashed silver and he smiled. His Alpha had turned into a damn monster since his mating with Aisling; he'd always been scary as fuck, but now he looked more frightening in his human shell than he did in his animal form - and that was saying a lot, given the fact that Rye turned into a damn saber-toothed tiger.

Daunte was grateful for his Alpha's freakishness; he loved his position as Beta, and he would have hated the responsibility that came hand in hand with being an Alpha, but he would never have been able to follow a weaker man. If it wasn't for Rye, he would have had to form his own pride, or become a loner. The former held no appeal; the latter was often a death sentence for a shifter. His sister had been a loner for a decade, and managed to thrive. But she'd never felt comfortable in their old pride, so leaving it hadn't been an ordeal for her. Daunte and his animal loved socializing. He played with the kids, joked around with the females, was the real life of the party. The loner life really wasn't for him. Thanks to Rye, he'd never have to experience it.

UNEXPECTED

*S*he'd won. The following Monday, an enthusiastic girl, with dark doe eyes and pastel makeup against her golden skin, was waiting for her in front of the bakery when she got in at five thirty.

Clari concentrated on the kid, so she didn't have to think about the grumpy, colossal, and overly sexy brooding figure leaning against the wall a step behind her.

"Hey, Niamh," Clari said, smiling at the kid, who practically skipped.

"Ace said it was your idea. She said you asked for me so I could get out of the pride house."

Her eyes gleamed at Clari.

"Sure did. Daunte was against it, though," she

smirked when the kid elbowed him in the abs. Finally acknowledging his presence, she spared him a glance while fiddling with her set of keys. "I thought Ian was supposed to be our assigned bodyguard?"

"We set up a schedule," he growled, everything about his stance making it clear that he was here against his volition.

Clari shrugged it off, refusing to let his reluctance bother her.

"You didn't have to be here this early. The bakery won't open until nine, you know."

Niamh grinned, "Sure, but Aisling said you bake the cakes at this time. If I can bake, you'll pay me more - plus I get to eat the rejects."

"Smart girl."

She'd found the right key, but the keyhole took a bit of fumbling; then, she had some trouble pushing the heavy duty door open. She could practically smell frustration emanating from the shifter behind her.

"You could let me…"

"I can manage," she snapped, not letting him finish that sentence. She'd opened the door by herself for months, at least five days a week – and, yeah, maybe it took so much effort that she considered it her daily workout, but she managed. She wasn't a helpless princess, and he didn't have a white horse or shining armor, dammit.

"Suit yourself. The view's certainly worth the wait."

Slowly, Clari turned her head to see that the dickhead was shamelessly staring at her ass - she *had* needed to bend down.

"Fine."

Glowering, she took a side step to give him the room to step in. Of course, the man pushed the door effortlessly, without breaking a sweat.

"You need to get that repaired before you pull a muscle."

She would genuinely have kneed him in the nuts if he'd said it in a condescending way, but he frowned, concerned.

"It's on the list," she shrugged. "Come on in. I'll show you to the staff waiting room – there are lockers for your personal belongings; no cellphone on you while you work."

She half expected a tantrum from Niamh, who seemed surgically attached to her iPhone, but she didn't bat an eyelash.

"I'd planned to give you a tour after we opened - right now, I need to start on the croissants, so you can either stay out of the way or…"

"I'll wash my hands. Let me know how I can help."

Well, what do you know?

THE PRESENCE of the obnoxious bodyguard strangely didn't bother her after a few minutes; in part because she was used to seeing him hanging out in the shadows without saying a word, and also because she was on *her* turf now. After a while, she managed to stop feeling self-conscious and got on with the work.

It soon became obvious that Niamh wasn't a stranger to baking; she did better than Clari had the first time Ace showed her her methods.

"'Fess up. You've done that before."

The teenager grinned.

"You know I was adopted into the pride, right?"

Clari nodded. All the children - except the baby Ace was currently carrying - had been adopted. She'd been curious at first, but she'd never asked for their backstory, feeling like it was something private. They'd share if they wanted to. It wasn't like she didn't understand; Clari was also pretty close to an adopted kid.

"I grew up on the streets, in another country. When I was young - very young - I realized I had powers and I used them to survive. I stole food, mostly. I think I was about ten when I had to defend myself, though."

Clari froze, dumping a ton of frosting on the cake she was working on. She'd had to defend herself at *ten?* From what? From whom? Children shouldn't have to even think about that - ever.

"It wasn't pretty. So, some agents of the PIA turned up."

Giving up on baking overall, she pulled a seat and planted Niamh on it, before rushing to the coffeemaker, and starting a hot chocolate. It felt like a story that needed to be accompanied by hot chocolate.

The PIA stood for the Paranormal Investigation Agency, and, even as a human being, Clari knew they were a big deal. When some big stuff happened because of sups - vampires, shifters, witches, angels, and other paranormal beings - they stepped in. Normally, you never heard about the perpetrator again.

"Go on," she urged.

"I got lucky. They could have sent a normal agent - I'm sure they *would* have, actually - but instead, someone from one of their special units arrived within minutes; in time to save the kids who were trying to hurt me, so I never murdered anyone." Niamh accepted the hot chocolate, and then Daunte took the one she'd made on autopilot.

"A special unit?" Clari asked.

"Yeah, normally their field agents just *take care* of the problem when a sup messes up. That means asking us to surrender - which is impossible when you lose control that way. Then, they can use deadly force. But, instead of an agent, I got Tria. She's part of a research department. I think she filed a report saying that an artifact malfunctioned, or something. I have no clue how she got me over here - it can't have been legal. She let me stay at her place for a few weeks, got me some papers, and then she asked me to get in touch with Rye."

Whoever this Tria was, Clari wanted to meet her and give her a hug.

"Anyway, she can't cook. Or bake. So, while I stayed there, I looked up some recipes and tried to make her favorite things. Maybe I thought if I did all that, she'd let me stay." She shook her head, and then changed direction. "It was weird, you know? Having as much food as I wanted in a fridge, and being able to do all these things with it."

Oh, the feels. A kid - a ten-year-old kid - who thought it was weird to have food? Clari was *never* going to give her sob story in front of Niamh. Never. Compared to that, it sounded like she'd been born with a damn silver spoon.

"When I moved to the pride, Ola let me help in the kitchen, too. I like it. If I could, I'd go to culinary school when I'm older."

"If you could?" Clari frowned, as Niamh pointed to her own chest.

"Witch. Before our kind are allowed to go to college,

we have to pass tests to evaluate how dangerous we are. Everyone knows that I'd be disqualified."

"Not necessarily," Daunte intervened, his dark chocolate voice reminding her of his presence. "You'll probably be classified as highly dangerous, yes; but if you prove that you can control yourself, the human authority can't stop you from living your life."

Niamh bit her lip, visibly restraining herself from stating the obvious; she wasn't on her way to prove anything if they didn't let her attend school, or meet anyone. Clari was just about to spell it out, when Daunte's phone interrupted.

"Cross," he said sharply.

He listened to the person on the other end for a few seconds, and then his face morphed into a mask of untold horror, becoming gray, green, and purple.

"Understood."

He hung up, and stared into the void, lost.

"What? What is it?" Niamh asked, concerned.

His lip quivered a little, before he pushed the words out of his mouth.

"Ace."

They both got on their feet, ready to run for it. Something happening to Ace was nothing short of inconceivable. She was so strong, larger than life, and there was an entire army of dominant shifters protecting her - not to mention her frightening mate.

Daunte held his hands up, gesturing them to slow down.

"No need to panic," he said, somewhat hypocritically. "But Ace is having the baby. Her water broke."

JUST A SCRATCH

"*S*top hogging him. I want my turn."

Daunte growled low, baring his teeth. No way was he relinquishing the small creature holding onto his finger. Blood of his blood. His perfect, perfect little nephew. He wasn't giving him up for anything, anyone. Not even her.

Clari meant business, arms crossed over her chest, glaring as menacingly as any human could, and his animal did acknowledge her, nodding his respect. But she wasn't taking Zackary from him. No one was.

"Oh, for Christ's sake, give her the baby, brother," Aisling growled.

Dammit. The one authority he couldn't actually ignore; his Alpha female - not to mention, the mother of the child. He sighed, walking closer to Clarissa; so close, in fact, that he could smell her intoxicating scent more clearly than he ever had.

"Be careful to hold the head," he told her softly, half expecting her to snap at him.

She just nodded and slowly, reverently, took the newborn from his arms.

He owed her, big time. She'd been his lifeline during the last ten hours. They'd closed the bakery and rushed to the pride house as soon as they'd heard the news, but there was no doubt that without her, he would have run for the hills within seconds.

Ace was screaming; long, agonizing screams loud enough to raise the dead. Hearing the first one, he'd practically vomited on the spot; at the second, he was ready to take a plane to the other side of the universe, but, just then, Clari had taken his hand, and Niamh's, too, before walking towards the entrance.

They'd waited in the living room with the rest of the pride, except for Rye and Ola. The Alpha and the Healer were in the room with Ace's doctors. She'd opted to have her child at home, like so many shifters did - particularly cats.

At each gut-wrenching scream, he damned her for it, wishing she'd gone to a hospital. Those yells would forever haunt the house; he was certain of it.

But finally, a high-pitched cry resounded, and the screaming stopped, replaced by tears and exclamations. Rye burst out of the infirmary, yelling, "A boy! We have a boy!" and there he was. Little Zack.

It was only at the end that he'd realized he was still holding on to Clari's hand, squeezing it hard.

"He's so precious," she breathed softly, smiling at the baby who grabbed a fistful of her silky hair.

The kid had good taste.

"I want one of these," Daunte said, suddenly finding himself foolish for even thinking that he wouldn't have a child. Of course he would. "Actually, make that a full litter."

"I pity the poor girl you choose as your incubator," Ace grumbled, before pointing her finger at Rye. "We're done. One perfectly nice baby is more than enough. Consider my ovaries retired."

"Hey, I don't want to seem rude, but is that normal?"

Everyone turned to Clari, and most of the pride stared open-mouthed. Ace laughed softly.

"That's definitely my boy," she said.

Zack had shifted. Instead of the adorable, smooth-skinned little human they'd all fawned over, there was a kitten in Clari's arms. A tiny little thing with a sable coat marred with small black spots. Let's face it; cats are cute. They needed to be, given the fact that they were absolute assholes. Being irresistible was part of their evolution, but never had Daunte

seen a cat quite as pretty as this one. The big dark
eyes, and his almost toothless grin, save for his two
front teeth, growing right under his upper lip, made
him the most enchanting creature to ever walk
this earth.

No one had expected that; children didn't shift -
normally, it started around puberty, or perhaps a little
earlier.

But he wasn't a typical shifter; he was son of Ace, the
hybrid born of a wild animal. She'd been born in her
feline form. They shouldn't have been astonished that
her own child wouldn't want to wait, either.

"Oh my god, look at him," Clari cooed as the lucky
little beast climbed up her shirt, his claws digging into
her breast, then nestled in the crook of her neck.

Eventually, all of them reacted.

They were too late.

"No!" that came from Daunte, just as Rye screamed,
"Careful!" and Ace yelled, "Pull him back!" Coveney,
Ola, Ian, Jas, and Christine, were all singing the
same tune.

But Zackary's saberteeth had already pierced Clari's
skin.

"Ouch."

They stared in silence. It wasn't like they automatically
had something to worry about. The odds were in their

favor. Clari probably wouldn't be affected at all; she'd just need a little band-aid, and that was that.

Right?

The chance was minimal. Only a tiny fraction of their kids were born with an infectious bite; perhaps a handful of children per decade. And they were taken care of before they got a chance to use their skills.

Shifters had a secret - a secret they couldn't afford to divulge. Humans were concerned with vampires, with angels, demon-born, and other larger-than-life creatures; all things considered, shifters weren't a threat to their existence. They generally kept to themselves, and when they didn't, their authorities took care of the problem.

But they were at the bottom of the list of threats because the humans didn't know that some amongst them were born with a sort of venom carrying their gene; a venom that could turn humans into shifters. Children were tested after their first shift - which generally meant after puberty - to check if they had it. They'd had zero reason to think Zack might have been a Turner.

"You wanna tell me why all of you are looking at me like I'm on my death bed? It's just a little scratch," Clari said, rolling her eyes, pulling the child back into her arms and rocking him.

"Hm."

"Errr-"

"Erumph."

No one wanted to break the news to her, it seemed, least of all the Alphas, who were probably feeling guilty for letting her close to Zack before doing their duty.

Well, it needed to be said.

"There's a zero point zero, zero, zero one percent chance that his bite might be venomous."

Clari stilled.

"So, what, I'm going to die if it is? There's an anti-dote, right?"

He shook his head.

"No, it's not lethal, per se." A half truth. "And no, there's no antidote."

She frowned, clueless.

In for a penny…

"If he's venomous, you'll change into one of us. You'll become a shifter."

HE DIDN'T THINK he'd ever felt as helpless as he did now, staring at the female. No, not female; *woman.* He wouldn't think of her as a shifter. Not yet. Not ever, if he could help it.

He'd said the affliction wasn't lethal. He'd lied. If she did turn, she would be killed. Perhaps not by the change itself - although not many were strong enough to survive it, according to what he knew about it - but she'd be hunted and killed by the Shifter Council. That was what they did to the children who could turn humans, that was what they did to the witnesses, and the proofs. Their secrets kept the bulk of their race safe from humanity's paranoia, and they'd do anything to ensure it was never revealed.

They needed to tell her, although she'd freak out. If she didn't know, she might do something stupid - like talk about it on social media. Daunte opened his mouth, and closed it.

Not yet. They would have to tell her soon - before she left the pride house - but he couldn't tell her yet.

"When will I know?" she asked in a whisper.

It was impossible to tell how she took the news by just looking at her. Clari's expression hadn't changed: she'd blanked out any feelings from her face.

"Within three to five days. We might be able to see some signs earlier."

Not even a week. In less than a week, they'd know.

PLAN OF ACTION

"*Y*ou're kidding me."

They were joking, right? That wasn't possible. Humans were humans, and that was that. They could be turned into vampires, they could even learn to use magic if they had a drop of witch blood… but they couldn't be *turned* into a shifter.

Pop culture had shown plenty of humans changed after a werewolf bite, but when they'd come out of the shadows thirty years ago, shifters had laughed at it. Since, they had seen plenty of proof that it was nothing but a myth, when stupid humans who'd provoked shifters into a fight had ended up with bite marks that hadn't changed anything about them.

"Do you really think any of us would joke about that?" Ace asked softly.

She got up from the sofa with some difficulty, and walked to her; Clari moved to reluctantly give Zack back, but she shook her head.

"It's not like a second bite would make any difference. He either is a Turner, or he isn't. Let me just have a look." Her hand touched Clari's neck, and retreated just as quickly. "It's not very deep, but he broke the skin."

Most members of the pride cursed at that.

"A Turner?" Clari repeated the unfamiliar term, trying to wrap her head around what was happening.

The tension was palpable and she could almost feel everyone exchanging glances, murmuring around her. Shit. Okay, so, maybe they weren't kidding. Maybe it was possible. That meant she needed to ask questions - a fair bunch of them. Like, what sort of odds were they talking about? What would happen to her if she did, in fact, turn, would she be accepted in their pride? Clari knew just how selective they were - they'd spent the last few months reviewing applications and didn't seem any closer to including even one new member. From what she'd learned about it from Ace, she knew she didn't want to be a loner; Ace had survived it, but Clari had no clue how to do the shifter thing.

Suddenly, she froze, one resounding question muting everything else. She'd never heard of a human turned by a shifter. *Ever.* That meant…

"That's a secret, right? The fact that you can turn us. You keep it secret."

Rye was the one who answered.

"Yes. The Shifter Council has unanimously opted to keep the matter under wraps. One of the only things every race has agreed on."

She bit her lip, pretty certain they hadn't just done a pinky swear.

"What's going to happen to me?"

It came out as something close to a whisper, and she hated it. She didn't think she'd ever sounded as weak, or as frightened.

Rye and Ace looked at her with pity, and she could guess what the silence meant.

"Oh, god. I'm going to die. You're going to have to kill me."

All of a sudden, she remembered a funny thing; almost ten years back, she and her cousin had been on vacation at the beach. They'd met a few shifters, and she could hear Lana's voice saying, "One day you'll get yourself in trouble if you don't stop mingling with their kind, Clarissa."

Funny how she'd felt like her cousin was just a silly privileged girl, at the time. Someone who never had to work for acceptance, and refused to give the benefit of the doubt to anyone who wasn't exactly like her.

She could almost hear Lana laughing at her now.

"Let's get one thing straight," a deep voice interrupted her inner pity party, and, when she lifted her eyes, Daunte was just in front of her, invading her personal space. "None of us - not *one* of us - will lay a hand on you. You got it?"

His amber eyes had changed to a gold shade, as Ace's did when she was pissed. She'd never seen his shift that way though. Clari gulped and bobbed her head.

"And you're not the only one the law would condemn," he added, pointing towards the baby now sleeping in her arms.

Her eyes bulged. They'd hurt a kid? No way! They couldn't.

"Hopefully, nothing will come of it. Turners are extremely rare."

"But what if he is one? What then?" she insisted. She couldn't just let it go, even if the probability was minimal. She needed to know, if only to prepare herself.

Rye was the one who replied.

"If he is one, and you turn, your body and mind will suddenly be forced to become something else. You'll change in every way. You may hate it. You may love it. You won't understand it. But we'll be here to guide you. If you shift, you'll be a Wyvern."

There were nods of assent all around.

She didn't know just how tense she had been until her shoulders sagged in relief. She wasn't going to be expected to deal with all that alone. Of course not. She felt a little silly for even thinking of it.

"But, the law…"

"No one will think to test Zack for years. As long as we're careful - which means never letting him out of sight, never letting him close to a human being - they'll never know what happened. When the council sends someone to see him… well, we know a few witches. I'm sure we'll find a workaround."

That sounded good, right?

"As for you- that could get complicated. Your friends, family- everyone will need to carry on thinking that you're what you've always been until now. That would take a lot of self-control on your part. Never showing your true nature. But with training, there's no reason why you won't manage."

Clari had smiled. Okay, that didn't sound all that bad, did it? In fact, if she was entirely honest, if only to herself, she didn't mind the idea of shifting.

Not at all.

"In the meantime, you're going to have to stay here, under observation for the rest of the week. The first shift is always the worst. We can close the bakery; with Zack's birth, no one will question it."

CATCHING A BREAK

*I*t took a lot to get a shifter drunk, but Daunte was doing his best to try, pouring one brandy after the next. He needed it, if only for a night. Maybe then, he'd manage to stop thinking. About *her*.

There was a very, very good chance that nothing had changed. She was just a normal, human girl, and she would remain so. But telling himself that, repeating it, almost chanting it, didn't change what he and his cat wanted.

Until then, they'd both been reasonable. They wanted her, but it was just a passing fancy he could get over. Relationships between humans and shifters could work, but not when the male was as dominant as he was. He needed a female strong enough to push back, or a submissive who understood the rules enough to fold under his demands; humans didn't get what their animal counterparts demanded; they could push, and push, ignoring the dominance, and end up getting hurt in the process. Daunte didn't think he was able to ever lay a hand on a woman, but he wasn't about to question facts that had defined his race for hundreds of years. Their animals could burst to the surface in anger when provoked.

Now that she'd been bitten, there was a possibility, a minuscule, quasi-nonexistent possibility, that she might have been turned and he entertained the idea. Clari in his arms. Clari's hand in his. Clari smiling up at him. Clari panting underneath him.

So, yeah. He fully intended to get drunk until it passed.

He genuinely didn't think anything could improve his sour mood until the phone in his pocket beeped. Pulling it, he frowned at the unknown number, until he read the text.

Nice day in Mexico.

That managed to get a smile out of him. Emily. It had to be Emily, telling him she was safe - or at least, alive. If she was smart, and he was pretty sure she was, she wasn't anywhere near Mexico. But she was well enough to send him a message, and that was what mattered. He hadn't abandoned her to her death.

"Wow. Daunte Cross smiling. I didn't think that was possible."

If he hadn't imbibed a dozen brandies, he would have heard and smelled her before she could get too close.

Daunte put the phone back in his pocket, and turned to face Clari.

Fucking hell!

"What are you wearing?"

She looked down at herself, before rolling her eyes.

"They're called PJs, Cross. Can't be the first set you've seen."

It wasn't. But Clari generally wore jeans and blouses, or pretty, conservative dresses that didn't show too much skin, reaching one inch below the knee. Her PJs were micro-mini stripped shorts, and a tight tank top that she wore without a damn bra.

Fuck.

"I had to borrow it from Ola," she admitted. "We'll stop at home tomorrow, after my aunt and uncle go to work."

He smirked; sure, the outfit wasn't as revealing as what most of the pride females wore, but it still wasn't her, and he'd been able to tell.

"You totally wear long pants. With giraffes on them."

"Pigs, I'll have you know," she replied good humouredly.

He hadn't spoken to her until the previous week, yet he knew her. How fucking weird was that?

"You live with your aunt and uncle?" he pried.

"Yep. My mother is a career woman. She got her big sister to raise me until I was in my teens; by then, I figured out I preferred my aunt's home. She's awesome - and her husband rocks. You've met them, I'm sure. He's the mayor."

That rang a bell.

"The guy who got this place built for his daughter? But then she went and married someone in the city, I think."

"Yes, Lana. She was never going to stay, but they did their best to make Lakesides appealing to her."

She said it without even a little bit of bitterness, but he read between the lines. Lana, the golden daughter they wanted, while she was just the niece, the guest. That explained a lot. He'd seen that she hadn't seemed to have much of a life outside of running the bakery, and she hadn't seemed to want to go home right away. Daunte had cursed her for coming to his home every day, taunting him; now he felt like an ass.

"You came home when she wouldn't. You moved back so they aren't alone."

She bit her lower lip and looked away, uncomfortable.

"Maybe. Is there anything to drink? Tea, coffee?"

"Caffeine? It's two in the morning."

She shrugged, making her breasts rise and fall in a way that was all too distracting.

"Can't sleep. I do have the whole *you may very well cease to be human in a couple of days* thing hanging over my head, you know."

The girl had a point. He lifted his glass.

"Brandy?"

ALPHAS

The circular room with animals painted on the light-yellow walls, was entirely littered by fluffy toys, and piles of presents they hadn't gotten around to opening yet. All their allies had sent gifts to little Zack. Their baby.

Five years ago, if someone had told him it was possible to feel so entirely whole and content, Rygan Wayland wouldn't have believed a word of it. His mate was rocking their treasure in her arms, absentmindedly humming a timeless lullaby. The picture of happiness.

Yet, he'd never been as wary, either, and he could see a shadow underneath Aisling's eyes that said she felt exactly the same. She'd blocked him through their bond; in the past, she'd only done it when she'd been furious - or hiding a birthday present from him. Now…

She was scared. Try as she might, she could never quite hide anything from him. They were two parts of the same soul.

"We have no reason to freak out yet," he voiced. "Turners are extremely rare."

His words felt empty, even to his own ears. Turners were rare because they came from old families descended directly from the very first shifters - witches had rendered the following generations unable to affect human beings.

But he was a Wayland; his family tree could be traced right back to the top, hence why he turned into so bestial an animal. And she? She was the very definition of a first generation of shifter. Part beast. He'd always been proud of everything she was, but there was no denying that it made their odds look grim.

"I feel danger coming, Rye. I can almost taste it."

He would have loved to say that he didn't; but that would have been a lie.

"Hsu would…"

"Hsu is a child. We shouldn't rely so heavily on her. For one, that could make us complacent. We…"

She stopped talking as a discreet knock interrupted them.

Opening the door, Rye tried to smile as best he could.

"Hey, little one. We were just talking about you."

The child had been crying. That much was obvious, although she'd done her best to hide it, drying her tears and lifting her chin. Her eyes were still red and puffy.

"What is it, sweetheart?"

"I'm sorry," she sniffed.

Those words seemed to undo her hard work; she lost her composure and started bawling her eyes out again.

"Hey, hey, now," he said, effortlessly lifting her from the ground like she was a toddler, too.

At ten years old, the girl rarely accepted that sort of comfort, but she buried her arms in his neck and cried harder.

"What is it, Hsu?" Ace asked, suddenly by their side.

She'd put Zack in his bed; from the corner of his eye, Rye could see the little monster immediately shifting and tearing through the curtains in an attempt to climb out. "You know you can tell us anything."

"I did something - something really bad."

"Right. Do I need to get a shovel to hide the body?"

Hsu didn't laugh, but the joke worked nonetheless; a reminder that they had each other's back, no matter what.

"I... I saw something last week, and I didn't tell. I

tried, and tried to stop seeing it, so I wouldn't have to lie."

Rye caught Ace's eyes flickering to his for an instant, but they went back on the child.

"Well, now, that doesn't sound too bad, does it? You know you don't need to share all your visions, Hsu. No Seer is supposed to. If you constantly meddle with the future, you're just going to get tired, and anxious, and you'll feel guilty when you *miss* something…"

Ace stopped her tirade, catching on at the same time as Rye.

"You saw this. You saw Zack biting Clari."

A head of dark curls bobbed against his chest. Oh boy.

"And you saw Clari turn," Rye concluded softly.

It took a minute, but she nodded again.

Knowing she could feel the beat of his heart underneath her, Rye did his best to control it and stay calm, wishing very hard that he was alone in the room, so he could yell every variation of fuck that came to mind, and throw something.

"Sweet pea," Ace said softly, still caressing her head, although her amber eyes shone bright gold, "you should have told us, because Clarissa might be in trouble now. But you know that."

Good, she'd managed to say it without yelling. Sometimes, he *loved* being able to share his responsibilities.

"I know, but Clari was *happy* in my vision. We all were. Everyone, even Zack was all grown up, and we were dancing under a big gazebo, before we all shifted. Niamh was there, dressed like a princess, all in gold. It was a *good* vision."

That didn't sound all that bad…

"But?" Ace asked, interrupting him just as he was about to tell Hsu that it didn't matter.

"But I can't see it now. I ignored my visions for a few days, and now, whenever I try, they're blocked. I can't see the party. I can't see anything, except *them.*"

Realizing she made no sense, the child lifted her hand and placed her fingers near Rye's temple, before sharing what she'd seen.

At first, she sent an image of the living room, where most of the members of the pride were standing in a wary stance that made Rye think they expected an attack. The children, in the centre of the room, were protected by most of them; a few amongst them were missing - presumably stationed elsewhere. What surprised him was that he saw a handful of unfamiliar faces. But at each image she sent after that one, he became more somber.

First, the Vergas Pack - an enemy who'd long waited

for the chance to get back at them. Rye could see the glee emanating from their psychotic Alpha as he paced around the border of their territory. Secondly, the Royal Pride, headed by one of the Enforcers - his father's man. That was already over a hundred enemies, and it was only the start. Right after, he saw the skies clouded by gigantic eagles, gorillas running through their woods, arctic bears coming from the lake, and worst of all: a dozen severe, clean-cut officers wearing black and green.

The birds, the gorillas, the bears- all those were rare, and directly protected by the Shifter Council, so long as they swore their allegiance, but Rye could have believed it a coincidence, if it hadn't been for the last group.

Those military trained shifters in green were the members of the Council.

Which meant that their entire race had declared war against them.

And they wouldn't survive it. They couldn't.

He wasn't sure he wanted to see more of Hsu's premonition this time, but, just when he was about to tell her he'd had enough, something pushed him back, hard, and his mind returned to Zack's sunny room.

"What was that?" he asked, confused, a headache rapidly forming.

And shifters practically never got headaches.

He'd seen red; actually, black and red. A slow, cloudy, tainted mist covering the entire vision- and then, nothing.

"I don't know," Hsu whispered. "But I can't see past that. I can't see."

A DELIGHTFUL VIEW

The knocking on her door was insistent, unforgiving, and she was pretty certain she growled. Someone giggled outside her door before opening it. Dammit. She should have locked herself in.

"You'll thank me for waking you up, and never question my judgement again, trust me on this."

She had serious doubts, on both accounts, especially when the intruder pulled her blackout curtains open, making her groan and hide under her pillow.

The traitor then went after her comforter. She yelled and kicked out, delighted when her feet hit something. She hoped it hurt.

"Dude, it's one in the afternoon."

"I was up until five in the morning."

Drinking Brandy. With Daunte.

As she was a lightweight, Clari never drank enough to pass out or be confused by what had happened; she remembered it clearly. For once, though, she wondered if her mind had played tricks on her. Because last night had been… nice. They'd talk about everything and nothing, like old friends. Daunte supported the Jaguars, while she preferred the Arctic Bears - because there was something poetic about seeing super-duper hot grizzly shifters in tight sports gear. He liked to listen to jazz, while she had a thing for pop. They both liked stupid movies featuring super heroes, rather than serious stuff. And when he was growing up, his sole purpose had been annoying the shit out of his big sister, because he loved when she was grumpy. He'd also been fiercely protective of her, getting into a fair amount of fights with those who talked shit about her for what she was.

"Then," he'd said, "when I was ten and hated by every kid in the pride, I met Rye at a Gathering. The Prince. I know you don't get our culture, but as far as we were concerned, he walked on water. He didn't have a lot of friends, even in his pride, and he rarely spoke to anyone; but he spoke to me. He friended me on social media and included me in his group. When we came back home, I was the cool kid, and they finally left Ace alone. I couldn't stand the hypocrisy of it all, but at the end of the day, no one bothered her."

She hadn't known anything about Daunte, except

the fact that he was hot as sin, and hated her guts; now she saw his defining quality was how protective he was of his family; which explained why he was Beta.

They'd drunk some more after that.

But Tracy didn't seem to care about the fact that Clari's head was pounding like it harbored a herd of elephants running from a T-Rex.

"I wasn't going to tell you anything," the female Enforcer said, "because I didn't want to ruin the surprise for you. But there's a dozen GQ-model-worthy shifters sparring in the gardens. Sweating. And mostly naked."

Oh. Right.

"In that case, I need clothes and an aspirin."

In under two minutes she was out the door, and blessing Tracy's devilish soul.

The entire pride stood under their gazebo, Ace and Rye standing at the front. They were all observing as a group of shifters were tearing each other apart before their eyes.

As Tracy had said, there were a dozen men, all of whom did seem to belong on the cover of a shiny magazine; sculpted, defined bodies glistening in sweat. There also were four women, just as beautiful.

"Rye has invited the top potential recruits today,"

Tracy whispered to bring her up to speed. "These are the fighters. The others are coming in a few weeks."

"Tracy, I owe you. Big time."

The Wyvern shifters were hot, of course, but Clari was used to them – and, except for Daunte, none of them made her feel all tingly. These new guys, though; every single one of them was drool worthy. Probably because she hadn't heard them speak yet.

Her eyes danced from one Adonis to the next, before settling on the tallest one; a larger-than-life blond hunk with long hair that fell down his shoulders, and tribal tattoos on his back, making him look like a damn Viking. He stopped two guys from launching at him by holding their heads back; when a third attacked from his side, he effortlessly lunged in the air and dropped kicked him, before shifting in mid air. She'd spent enough time googling different breeds of wild cats since the Wyvern's arrival to recognize his spotted fur and his facial markings immediately. He was a Cheetah, although his body was larger than the standards in the wild, there was no mistaking the features.

"Luke Hall. And yes, his family originates from Scandinavia," Tracy whispered to her ear. "I got Ian to online stalk him as soon as he got in."

"He's in, right?"

"It takes more to be included in this pride than a set of muscles," Ian replied haughtily.

74

Most of the guys acquiesced.

"Well, maybe but he still has my vote," Ace piped in, making every male groan and Rye bite her earlobe. "What?" she shrugged. "Being mated doesn't stop me from having eyes."

"Behave if you don't want me to start using my eyes to look at other females," Rye teased, earning a growl.

After a few minutes, Rye stepped forward, calling, "Enough."

The fighting ceased gradually. One of the guys who'd ganged up on Luke Hall puffed his chest and carried on advancing towards him, but another one held him back, and he dropped it with a sigh. The women were the last to stop. As for the hot giant, he'd stopped immediately, and dropped to his knees. His crouch was fascinating; one knee folded under him, another one against his chest, and the tip of his fingers pushing against the ground. It could almost have looked like a submissive stance, but he actually seemed ready to pounce within seconds, in any direction.

"Look at everyone, try to get an impression on them," a low voice whispered in her ear.

Daunte. He'd been up front with Rye when she first arrived, but although she hadn't seen him move, here he was, right behind her.

"The pride will speak about each potential later. You might see something we've missed."

"I'm not exactly part of the pride," she reminded him.

A dozen pair of eyes turned to her, cautioning her.

Oh. Maybe she couldn't speak about her predicament in front of strangers.

"Nevertheless. You'll be there tonight, so look. At everyone."

He didn't need to say *and not just that hot Viking* out loud.

She wasn't sure what possessed her to say, "Hey, I'm *not* mated, *and* I have eyes. I'm doubly allowed to leer."

She wasn't sure what reaction she'd been hoping for; a laugh, perhaps. But she really, really hadn't expected Daunte to pull her arm, bend forward to reach her, and nip at her ear, just like Rye had done to Ace a few minutes ago.

"What do you think you're doing?"

Clari was glad her voice came out badass and menacing.

"Making you blend in. You stand out like a sore thumb."

Protests died on her lip at the annoyingly flawless reply.

"Well, as long as it is understood that I hated every second of it."

She felt his chest move as he chuckled against her back.

"Keep telling yourself that, sweetheart."

PROSPECTS

uck. Her scent. Her soft, tanned skin. The soft locks he felt against his face.

He shouldn't have done that. He really shouldn't have, but he knew there was no going back.

Clari's heart skipped a beat and she gasped. But she didn't push him. She didn't tell him to stop. She didn't turn around and slap him, asking how he dared touch her without her assent. Which meant she wanted him. He'd known she wasn't indifferent to him, but he'd never asked himself if she'd welcome his advances, for his own sanity. Now, he knew.

But in four days, they'd be back to square one, and she'd be nothing more than a human woman. Precious and breakable. For both of their sakes, he needed to forget that knowledge. Take a step back. Leave her alone. Learn to ignore her again.

He stayed put, keeping his hand on her arm posses-sively, a gesture letting every stranger in their garden know she was his.

"I thank you for this display. Your skills allow each and every one of you to pass to the second round."

And without further ado, Rye shifted.

Daunte was proud when he saw that Clari didn't move, or shiver.

The outsiders were another story. Ten of them yelled, some stepped back, others stepped forward, ready to attack. To be fair to them, Rye *was* monstrous. Taller, longer, thicker than any other feline shifter Daunte had ever met, the tiger also sported those huge, curving canines, coming out right under his upper lip. To Daunte's knowledge, it was a family trait, but not all of them were born with that gene.

Rye shifted back, standing naked and indifferent to it; shifters couldn't be prudes. But everyone stared at the glowing tattoos on his skin, marking him for what he was: an Alpha mated to his fated mate. Twice as powerful as he had been before Ace.

"Great. Those of you who stepped back can go home; the rest of you, get dressed and come on in. We'll proceed to the rest of the tests when we get home."

Daunte waggled a brow, surprised. He was pretty cer-tain most members of their pride had freaked the first time he'd shifted. He wasn't the only one to find it unfair.

"Wait, so that's it? We're rejected, just like that? There's nothing wrong with being startled," one of the woman said.

"No, there's nothing wrong with it. But truth is, I'm a freak. So is my mate. And her brother."

"I resent that," Daunte interjected.

"And our son. Not to mention some of our children. There will be things happening in this pride - things you may not see anywhere else."

Daunte froze. So, that was what it was about. Clari and Zack. Rye wanted to get rid of the faint of heart because they'd be the first to panic in case she changed.

"Trust me: if my tiger freaks you, you can't deal with us. The rest of you, get dressed and come on in."

The bulk of the applicants walked towards the entrance of the property, muttering dejectedly. The rest of the pride got inside.

Daunte caught Rye by the arm right before they passed the threshold. He closed the door behind Ian, to get some privacy for a second. Shifter hearing could be a pain.

"I don't get it," he whispered. "Last week, you

wouldn't hear about getting reinforcements, then all of a sudden, you call a meeting within twenty-four hours. All of us got spooked by your tiger at first, but you'll only consider those who aren't… Isn't it a little premature?"

It sounded like Rye was preparing for war, and Daunte didn't like it - mostly because Rye hadn't shared his reason with him yet.

And, alright, that might have been because he'd woken up late, and the strangers had already arrived by the time he'd emerged downstairs. Damn brandy.

"I talked to Hsu," Rye replied.

Shit.

Hsu, a ten-year-old child who'd come to them close to four years ago, had visions; all of which had come to pass. They were always accurate, and generally just a hair short of apocalyptic.

"Is it Zack? Clarissa?"

He barely recognized his voice.

"Both," his Alpha replied. "She saw people come at them both. We were there, but there also were strangers getting in the way, trying to help them. I recognize some of their faces amongst these," he said, gesturing to the inside of the pride house. "None were those who stepped away from me, though."

Well, this explained that.

"Do they make it?" he asked. Hsu saw the visions evolving when they changed their path. "Do we all make it?"

Rye just shook his head, looking more tired than ever.

"I don't know. There's a block. She can't see anything past a certain event, in just a few weeks. Something shielded from her gets in the way. That can be good, or bad. For now, all we can do is try to make it until then."

Daunte nodded, and started asking how he could help, until something hit him. He should have thought of it sooner, but with everything Rye had just revealed, he'd just caught up.

"That means she's going to shift. Clarissa. She's one of us."

And Zack was a Turner. But right now, his heart beating at a thousand times a minute, he was concentrating on the first part of the equation. It felt like, in the middle of all this turmoil, someone had sent him a lifejacket to hold on to.

The woman he'd wanted more than anyone else in the world was going to become strong enough for him to make her his.

Well, if she'd have him; given the fact that he'd been an asshole to her for the last ten months, he couldn't exactly rely on that.

"Yes. Poor girl. She had a normal life until now. Now,

she's going to have to lie to everyone she cares about, and relearn everything she thought she knew."

INSIDE, Daunte paid attention, watching closely as Rye observed the candidates left. Some, he barely paid any mind to - others, he stared at intensely until they squirmed and looked away.

Interesting that he already knew who he was going to pick - the entire selection process was just for show. It wouldn't do for an Alpha to seemingly pick his pride members at random.

Tell me the poser wasn't in the vision, Daunte texted Rye, as the mountain of muscles happily removed the shirt he'd just put on to show his tattoos to the women.

"Some of them are decorative, but, this one, I got the first time I survived a hunt - in England, Huntsmen still hunt our kind."

Jas giggled, pointing to another design. "And that one?"

Daunte was going to barf. And possibly also punch the guy in the teeth, if Clari started to giggle, too.

He was, the Alpha replied immediately, accompanying his message with a shake of his head, making it clear how enthusiastic he was to welcome Luke.

"So, you left your family to be mercilessly hunted and came over here," Ian summarize merrily.

The giant shrugged.

"No, they're all dead."

Oh, great. Now, they were the assholes.

LIES

$\mathcal{N}$o one said anything for a beat after the hunk had served Ian a curveball.

"How did they die?" Clari asked, because it appeared that no one else was nosy enough to do it.

A few Wyvern shot her a reproachful look; but if this was about trying to find new members for their pride, they needed to know the basics.

"Not because of Huntsmen, strangely enough. There're worse things in the world. Well, in his wisdom, my brother offended one of those *worse things*. A Scion."

She was relieved to see that just about everyone seemed as clueless as she was.

"Sorry, I'm not familiar with the term."

Luke scratched his chin, trying to find his words.

"There are a few words for them - you may call them differently. The Descendants, maybe?"

Ace, Ian, and Tracy seemed to understand.

"But I thought they were myths?" the young novelist said. "You know," she told the rest of the pride. "The children of actual deities. We're not talking Demi-Gods, although those are rare enough. You take two full-fledged gods, make them have a baby - that's a Descendant. Or a Scion, I guess."

Clari's head was going to spin. Gods? Actual, real life, gods? They were a thing? She attempted to keep her expression even, not sure if she was supposed to act like the clueless human she was in front of strangers.

"There are, perhaps, a hundred Scion in this world. Some of them are just a little stronger than warlocks, but there are some who can make as much damage as a volcano by flipping their fingers. Brother dearest stole the girl of one of the latter kind."

"If you have a quarrel with one of them, we might not be in a position to accept you," Ace told him. "We have kids to think about."

Luke shook his head.

"Ajax let me go. No quarrel there. He said I was to live my life and be a reminder of what happened to those who defied him. I'm welcome to share the story - in fact, he demanded it. Which is ever so slightly deranged and plenty megalomaniacal, if you ask me, but, as it saved my skin, I'm not in a position to complain."

No one added anything for a while.

"Well, that was rather cheery, wouldn't you say?" the only woman left piped in. She was a pretty thing, only just taller than Ace, with dark curls and long lashes. "While I'm just here because my damn Alpha is trying to get in my pants and my Beta of a father is all for pimping me. Did I mention he's twice my age?"

"Gross," Tracy grimaced.

"Double gross," Ace echoed, turning to a slender, and mostly quiet male whose keen eyes took in everything.

"What's your story?"

"Youngest brother. Why can't I be as dominant, as handsome, as fast as my perfect elder brother - blah blah. I need out of the family pride."

"Oh, you're plenty hot enough," Tracy said, batting her eyelashes.

And he was. Compared to the muscle men in the lounge, he may very well be the slimmest, but he would have stood out in any other crowd.

"You?" Rye asked the last remaining contender, a broad man in his early thirties, like the Alpha.

"I was raised in a Lion's Den," he replied with distaste. Another thing Clari didn't quite understand - she stored it in a corner of her mind; she'd ask, or research it at the first occasion. "Now that my father's passed, the females expect me to take his place. At least half a dozen of those females are my half sisters."

She wrinkled her nose, hoping it wasn't what it sounded like.

"So, you all have reasons to want to be out of your current situations, and reasons to remain faithful to the pride. That's a good start, but I need more than that. Each and every one of us is loyal, not because we need to be, but because we're family. You need to be able to show that you want to be part of this family. We also need to decide which role you can fill amongst us."

That sounded reasonable to Clari, yet at the same time, she stiffened, feeling quite uncomfortable. Was she going to have to pass all these tests before officially having a place in the pride, too? She bit her lip.

"So, here's the plan. There's a house that belongs to us a mile from here. You're going to stay there until we know we can trust you. Pridemates, this is Ariadna, Luke, Theo and Sawyer. Welcome them, and observe them. In one month, we'll discuss their permanent inclusion."

COVENEY TOOK the potential recruits to Ace's old house, leaving the pride alone.

"So, what's a Lion's Den?" was the first thing coming out of her mouth, and everyone groaned.

"Have you seen some nature documentaries about lions? It's one male, a bunch of females, and their cubs. Just *one* male. With a lot of pussies to satisfy. Well, some lion shifters run their prides that way. Before you ask, it's the females' choice. These groups are run by the females. Still… it's pretty disgusting. The poor guy they pick spends his days and night satisfying the females in heat. They're often heavy into incest."

She held her hand up.

"Right. Enough about it before I throw up; anyone wanna talk about something else? Anything else?"

As it turned out, someone did.

"Well, that was all rather sudden," Ian told Rye, in a tone that was just a hair short of accusatory. "I didn't know we were going to interview today."

"In the light of recent events, I've moved our schedule up," the Alpha replied.

Now she paid attention to him, Clari saw that he looked tired; so did Ace, come to think of it. Nothing surprising; they *did* just bring a little thing into the world within the last few days. She hadn't heard Zack cry at all, but she would have slept through a storm, considering the amount of alcohol she'd ingested.

91

"Recent events?"

Clari saw a passing shadow before Rye nodded.

Lie, she thought. He was going to lie.

Which was stupid. How would she know? She'd always been hopeless at poker.

"Zack's birth. It made me quite conscious of the fact that the nine of us can't hope to patrol around the clock efficiently. I'd feel more comfortable with more men around my son."

It sounded genuine enough. Why couldn't she stop thinking that it wasn't?

TOMORROW

The pride dispersed after the potential recruits' departure, Daunte, to patrol with Jas, others to return to their tasks; he knew Tracy had a deadline looming over her, which made her hide in her office and scream at her computer screen every other day.

When he came back to the pride house in the afternoon, a smile tugged on his lips as he took in the sleepy female bundled in on one of their largest sofas, not even pretending to watch TV.

"You're okay?"

Clari lifted her head and bobbed her head, holding a hand in front of her mouth as she yawned.

"Yeah, just really tired."

Of course she was. Cats always were.

He had so many things to tell her. *I'm sorry. Don't be afraid. You'll be fine. I want you.* He wasn't sure she'd find much comfort in any of that.

"I have no excuse, though. I slept like the dead for a good eight hours last night after all that brandy. Do you think it's that?" she asked, her hand flying to her throat.

The bite mark had been so shallow, made by the smallest of fangs, barely bigger than needles - it should already have practically disappeared. It hadn't. In fact, the two puncture scars looked a little bigger than the wound had been. If it had been benign, they wouldn't be there - Daunte tried to stay expressionless as he looked at the puncture marks.

"Maybe."

If maybe meant, yep, definitely.

"You know, with everything going on, I don't think anyone took the time to ask you how you felt about all that. Possibly becoming furry, you know."

Clari surprised the shit out of him when she broke into a smile.

"Well, that very much depends on what type of furry I turn into. I can deal with being a badass cute little munchkin like Ace."

Daunte chuckled, trying to imagine his sister's face if she'd heard that. The Alpha female loved Clari, but she might very well challenge her for the offense. She was *just a little* sensitive about the fact that she turned into a tiny little lynx-like cat, barely any bigger than a domestic cat.

"I can totally deal with being big and scary, or super fast. But if I turn into an overgrown sphinx submissive, I demand a redo."

He smiled indulgently, shaking his head.

"I read up on it. You'll turn into something similar to your maker - or a feline associated to his bloodline. That means, a Cross, or a Wayland. I don't think either of our families is weird enough to produce anything close to a sphinx. As for the submissive thing, that won't be determined by your change. You'll stay you. If you're a submissive now, you'll stay submissive."

She lit up at that.

"Ace thinks I'm very dominant. Unless she was just being nice."

She grimaced at the thought, and he wouldn't have that.

"She wasn't. Ace doesn't see being submissive as a flaw - none of us do. Do you think we'll think about any of our children as defective, if they grew up without the will to throw their dominance about? There's a certain balance in the world, thanks to submissives. Without them to keep the peace, to be the voice of reason, and to give us a reason why we shouldn't jump into a fight and leave them defenseless, we'd constantly be at war."

Clari seemed to think it through, and nodded.

"I see your point. And yet, your pride is full of dominants - everyone except Christine, right? And she just seems to stay to either take care of the kids or cook and tidy up. She doesn't seem to mind, and there's nothing wrong with that, but it's not me. And when you opened up new places, you only called for fighters."

He saw how she could have jumped to that conclusion, with a limited understanding about shifters.

"There's eight children in our pride, and just ten adults. That's nine members we need to take care of, and nine members trained to fight," he explained. "We're balanced. As for the try out today, Rye only called to the fighters, yes. Because, for one, it makes sense to measure them against their peers. But soon, we'll also be seeing the non-fighters. I looked through the applications, and amongst the ten people we've selected for that round, three of them are dominant. They can take care of themselves, but, then again, all of us can. Including the children. Including Christine. Try to pinch some food off her before she sets the table, you'll see what I mean. Her submissive status just means her first instinct isn't to jump at someone's throat."

He could tell he'd given Clari a fair bit to think of; there was a cute little wrinkle between her eyes. Daunte had a hard time resisting the urge to drop his lips on it.

"Fair enough," she conceded. "I guess it wouldn't be so bad, then."

As she'd come to respect both positions, he decided to put her out of her misery.

"Good. But Ace was right, you're dominant."

Humans, like every other mammal out there, could exude dominant vibes - they just couldn't feel them on a conscious level. He'd felt Clari's just fine, each time he'd been an ass and ignored her. She hadn't liked it, and her glare had been accompanied by distinctive pushes of her potent power, clearly stating, "try to piss me off any more, *just try it.*"

And yes. That had made him so fucking hard. Each time. She had no idea how much self restraint he'd needed to exert to give the impression of indifference.

She shot him *that* smile, the one she reserved for those who'd earned it, the one he'd fucking hated, because it was never directed toward him. Her chocolate eyes shone, brightening the entire room.

"Tell me more," she asked, and he did.

He told her about the various ranks in prides, the

authorities in place amongst the shifters, the systems humans had to keep them at bay; he even spoke of the time before either of them were born, when the sups had emerged out of nowhere - as far as humans knew, in any case.

Clari knew of the dark days - the Age of Blood - but she'd heard about it in a human perspective.

Vampires had been the first to come out. Some said they'd been selfish to reveal themselves that way without consulting other races, but Daunte wondered if they'd done it because they were some of the strongest creatures out there; they'd done it so that the entire paranormal community could have a chance to exist in harmony with humans.

Of course, it hadn't been all flowers and rainbows. At first, humans chose to attack - and they lost, almost overnight. Vampires ruled the lands, for a time, and, slowly, other sups revealed themselves; shifters were amongst the first.

The reign of vampires only lasted three decades; they earned a peace amongst witches, humans, and their kind, and swore to leave the rule of the world to mortals, as long as each race had a say.

"Technically, we're still under an oath. If humans take it too far, or if witches try to rule us, there's a good chance that the vampires will come back. Our dad fought in New York during the Age of Blood, and he says that's why he couldn't bring himself to shift back for a time. There are memories haunting him; vampires aren't evil, but they are cold, and the world was a dreadful place during their time."

Clari nodded.

"My aunt and uncle won't speak of it. They were young, and lived in the country at the time, so they can't have dealt with the witch war, like your dad, but they still refuse to tell us about it."

Daunte could imagine why.

Catching something that seemed odd again, in the way she just mentioned her aunt and uncle when they talked about family, he asked, "How about your own parents? Do they speak of it at all?"

She smiled. "First of all, this is not a pity party. I had an awesome upbringing."

Basically, that was the gracious way any pity party started, but he let it slide.

"My mother got pregnant with me during her summer break after high school. She'd just got a scholarship to Yale, full ride, and no one wanted her to miss out. She refused to have an abortion, though, so, she gave birth to me and her older sister took me in. The deal was, she was going to earn her degree and come back, but she's *smart*. After her bachelor's, she got a master's, and a PhD, after that. Then, she got a very important job in a lab - we're talking super secret, and seventy hours a week. So, I stayed with my aunt and her husband, who were awesome. My mother visits on holidays, and she's fun. She gives the best presents, and tries to force an allowance on me. Without success, I might add. But, yeah, I guess she isn't exactly my *mother*."

He nodded, seeing that while there might be some pain and resentment lingering underneath the facade, she'd been right. It wasn't a pity party at all.

"I get it. My mother raised Ace; they might not share blood, but she's her mom. Like your aunt is for you. And we haven't given birth to our kids, but they're ours. I may just be Zachary's uncle, but he's mine, too. Prides aren't blood, but they're family."

She smiled sleepily, and yawned again.

"I'm keeping you up. You rest," he said. "Tomorrow will be a long day."

She didn't question it, thankfully. He didn't want to have to tell her what he knew. What he smelled. What he saw in her eyes as they flashed red.

Tomorrow, she was going to shift.

FIRST SHIFT

*R*un. Run. Run faster.

Over the tantalizing smell of the woods, the soft grass under her paws, and the sound of the water running nearby, she caught a scent and bared her fangs, growling low. She didn't recognize it. It didn't belong here.

The feline pushed all her powerful musculature forward and shot through the trees like a cannon, until she was close enough to hear her prey clearly. Then, she climbed up a tree and waited patiently.

Stranger. Female. She didn't belong. She might hurt the cubs.

She looked at the hairless biped and saw her for what she was underneath her pretty smooth skin; another shifter. The woman walked forward, toward their den.

No! A stranger. The cubs… The feline jumped down with a roar, claws out.

"Please, don't!" the female screeched the words when she caught sight of her.

Just before she hit the stranger, a large flying object hit her at full speed, knocking her back.

No, not an object. She knew that scent.

"Sorry," the Beta was saying to the stranger. The feline bared her teeth. Why was he being nice to the intruder? "We're on high alert right now, and my pridemate wasn't expecting you. I recognise your face from our applications, don't I? If you are here for the selection, that was yesterday."

The stranger's heart beat fast. She was frightened. *Good.* The feline was grumpy at her Beta for stepping in between her and her prey, but it was his prerogative. She wasn't sure she wanted to obey her Beta, but if he protected the stranger, she wasn't a threat. Plus, the fact that the pretty girl was shaking made up for it.

"You want to follow that trail down, until you reach a mini McMansion. Our Alphas are at home. Go, I'll take care of this," he said, gesturing to her.

Meanwhile, the feline licked her claws clean, and stretched languorously. Oh. Stretching was just the *best*. The feline dropped to the ground and stretched harder.

"What am I gonna do with you?" the Beta asked, laughingly.

His mouth moved, sounds came out. She wasn't sure what it meant.

I know what it means.

The feline stilled. She knew that voice.

Let me help.

That was her hairless biped. Her human.

Let me out.

Clarissa. That was her name.

LET ME OUT.

The feline huffed in distaste. But she liked Clarissa. Clarissa needed to stay happy. So, slowly, she retreated to the shadows of their mind.

THE BONE BREAKING process was excruciating. She yelled. She didn't even feel guilty for yelling so damn hard it would have raised any dead buried in the wood. When it stopped, she was crouched on the ground, panting hard.

Eventually, she managed to talk.

"Holy fuck."

The speed. The power. The smell of *everything.* Every sound around her, magnified tenfold.

She loved it and it made her sick to the bone, with a migraine so hard her head was ready to explode.

"Holy fuck," she repeated.

A chuckle got her to snap into focus, her eyes stopped flying from branches to leaves, to the skies, and the ants on the ground. They went to him. And, suddenly, the rest faded.

"Sorry, we're gonna suck at giving you warnings." That voice was making her clit sing. So hot. *Talk again,* she wanted to say. He did. "We were born that way. The good news is, you'll get used to it. We're proof of that."

She still heard everything else, but the volume seemed to have dialled down. She had to focus, apparently.

"You're right."

Was that *her* voice? It sounded so clear. And what was it with the accent, damn it?

"You suck. A warning would have helped."

But she didn't care. She didn't care about anything right now - her mind focused on one single thing.

"Clarissa?" Daunte asked, no doubt catching something in her eye.

Or the fact that she couldn't stop staring at his crotch.

"Don't take it personally," she said, licking her bottom lip. "But I think I need you to fuck me now."

What. The. Hell.

Had she actually *said* that? She'd never been that forward. *Ever.* Yet the words had flown out of her lips like she was just saying hi.

"Sorry, I don't know what came over me…"

Daunte had stopped laughing; he looked at her intensely, without any humor in his amber gaze now.

"Do you take it back?"

Oh, that voice. Again. Right to her clit.

She shook her head. Daunte tilted his, slowly ogling her. It was only under this observation that she realized she was entirely naked.

Fuck.

Daunte took a step forward, slowly. And another one. And another one. When he was right in front of her, he lifted his hand to her neck, pushing her hair off her shoulder, uncovering her breast. The eager nipples stood to attention, begging for his mouth.

"You're a shifter, darling. You'll crave touch. You'll crave sex. You'll crave everything you've ever wanted a thousand times more."

That sounded about right.

"If it had been Coveney or Ian following you, you would still have begged to be fucked. I don't matter to your gorgeous, slutty pussy."

She wasn't sure how the hell she did it, but, the next second, she'd jumped up, wrapped her legs around his neck, and flipped him down on the ground.

"If you're gonna spout nonsense, might as well keep that mouth of yours occupied," she growled, her voice as cold as his, before shifting her hips forward and sitting on his face.

"There's a good boy. Eat."

To be entirely honest, she had zero clue what the fuck was happening; but she liked it. Especially when, after glaring at her for a good minute, Daunte opened his mouth, and flicked her folds with his tongue, arms around her thighs, holding them in place until she yelled.

Scratch him.

It wasn't words, not really, but she could feel what the creature inside her wanted just as clearly as if it had said it out loud.

Mark him.

That was stupid. Why would she hurt him?

Mark him.

The creature needed her to.

Clari remembered when she'd been locked in the darkness, unable to make her body move; she'd needed the animal to let her back, and she had. So, stopping herself from questioning it, she moved her hips down to his torso, and tore through the fabric of Daunte's shirt, uncovering his naked skin. Then, softly, she slid her finger down his muscles as her lips dropped down to his neck.

"I wouldn't have fucked anyone else," she whispered.

"Poetic."

He sounded breathless, a little stunned.

"But you're about to cross a line you don't understand, beautiful," he said, eying her right hand.

She saw her fingertips had been replaced by sharp claws. Strange. She hadn't even felt it.

"You see the mark Ace gave Rye? Scratch me with this, and it will be just as deep. Just as permanent. And I'll scratch you back."

Clari noted that he wasn't exactly telling her to stop, though. Which was crazy because they didn't know each other. Plus, he'd seemed to hate her not even a couple of weeks back. So yeah, no scratching.

Her cat hissed in protest.

"Enough of that," Daunte said.

And just like that, without any sort of momentum, he flipped them around, throwing her on her back.

"You know what you were doing, Clarissa?" he asked, forbidding. "You were taking control. You were demanding my submission. *Mine.*" The last word came out as a growl as his eyes changed, making her freeze underneath him. That didn't last long, but by the time she was kicking and screaming, he was holding both of her hands over her head, and practically sitting on top of her naked frame.

"And you almost had it, too, sweet. Almost. But this isn't how it's going to work. You're *never* going to try to bully me again." She hissed. Was hissing her thing, now? "And, in exchange," he added, "I'll return the favor. I won't make you open your mouth and take me without asking your permission, like you just did to me."

Oh. Well, said like that, she'd sort of been an asshole. And a half.

"Deal?"

She inclined her head in sign of agreement.

"Good. Now, if you'd please open your legs, I'll fuck you harder than you've ever been fucked, because, frankly, your display of dominance was as hot as it was infuriating."

Her mouth opened in shock as he smirked down at her. She'd genuinely believed he'd been pissed for a second. But it looked like he'd just messed with her to keep her on her toes - and to reassert his dominance.

Her cat was both impressed and calmed down by it; she didn't push the urge to take a chunk out of his arm now, in any case.

Glancing left, she saw that her hand was back to normal.

"Come on, sweetheart. We haven't got all day. And I can't wait to get inside you."

She parted her legs, and immediately moaned as he shoved a finger deep in her pussy without preamble.

RUNNING AWAY

Ola spent most of the afternoon with the kids, ignoring the strangers who wanted a place in this large, dysfunctional, yet beautiful pride. She loved every single one of them. She even loved Zack. How could she not?

But that didn't matter. Nothing did now.

She'd seen it with her own eyes - before Daunte rushed to rescue her like she was a damsel in distress. A gorgeous tigress who smelled like Clari. Or rather, what Clari would have smelled of if she hadn't been born human.

So, that was that. Zackary was a Turner.

There were reasons why Turners were killed - good ones, or no one would have condoned the slaughtering of children. It was a sacrifice for the greater good; one child in hundreds of thousands died so that their entire race may carry on living in peace, without being persecuted.

And that was what would happen to Zack. Because she'd seen war, she wouldn't let it be the fate of her entire race out of attachment. She couldn't.

No one paid attention to her leaving. Rye was a good Alpha, not too controlling. She was allowed to come and go as she pleased, when she wasn't on an assignment. But they might have noticed that she was carrying a large suitcase, if they hadn't been distracted by Zack, the potential new recruits, and the news that Clari and Daunte had mated.

Ola was lucky she got away, though. She knew there was a chance Hsu might have seen - and prevented - her departure. Not that it would make any difference. She'd already sent an email to the Shifter Council. She was only leaving because, if she didn't, there was no doubt that the members of the Wyvern Pride would kill her for what she'd done.

Her car just passed the borders of their territory; she breathed out in relief.

She'd made it.

Then, all of a sudden, an all too familiar silhouette appeared in the middle of the road.

Shit. *Shit.*

She can't stop the car, Ola told herself. She hit the accelerator, driving at high speed.

The woman didn't move at first; then, she started running *towards* the moving vehicle.

What the hell?

Before her astounded eyes, Ola saw Aisling Cross-Wayland jump up to the hood of her car, then heard her land on the roof. With a single punch, her first tore through metal, and her claws sliced through it like it was made of cardboard.

The Alpha female grabbed her by the throat as she screamed.

"I'm glad it's you. I liked you the least," she told her, before punching through her ribcage and clawing her heart out.

Ace jumped down from the car before it swerved out of control, and disappeared into the woods.

THERE WAS NO DENYING IT, no words needed to try to justify it. Clari was his. She may not have been born his fated mate, but she'd been changed into it. Her dominance level was equal to his - which meant she'd win when she pushed, he'd win when he did; but, together, they were going to be perfect. Eventually.

Like, *not* half an hour after her first shift when she had zero clue what world she'd been launched into.

He'd claim her - or she'd claim him - soon enough. Hopefully, not right now.

He undid his fly and placed his hard dick right at her entrance, before pushing it in with a grunt as the wet, hot folds took him all in. Fuck. Was it supposed to feel like this? He pulled out, and thrust in again, hard, fast, entirely without volition. Releasing her arms, his hands found her ankles and pulled them onto his shoulders to get even deeper inside, angling his body until he hit a spot that made her beg for release.

It wasn't pretty. It didn't last long. Hard, fast, and primal, their first mating was about relinquishing control. If they hadn't done it, their animals would have been driven to the brink of madness. They needed it. Just like their human counterparts.

"Please," she begged, as he pinched her clit between his fingers.

He could barely see a thing, his vision blurred, all his senses fading, leaving nothing but this. But them.

Funny how he'd told her off, and stopped her from marking him, yet now, almost over the edge, he yelled out in frustration, willing everything in him to stop himself from marking *her.* He knew all the reasons why he shouldn't.

Fuck reason.

"Clarissa?"

Her eyes snapped into focus, watching him with attention, as her breasts bounced with each of his thrusts.

"Come here. Mark me now."

She didn't hesitate, dropping her legs to each side of him, and sitting up without breaking their insane rhythm. Both her hands reached around his back and clawed from just above his shoulder blades, while he bit down on her shoulder, hard. He fucked her right through their first orgasm, his dick never going down. And again. And again.

Eventually, he scented an intruder. Ian.

"Erm. Rye asked me to check on you. The second wave of applicants is here and-"

"Busy."

The growl had come from Clari. His mate. And he was, indeed, busy fucking her from behind.

"I see that. Well, shall I tell him you'll be along…"

"Get the fuck out of here, Ian," he growled, panting hard.

Not that he cared about him seeing them. At all. Let everyone see Clari was his. Everyone.

It was nightfall when they fell on the grass. She immediately went to sleep, but he caressed her hair and licked at the mark that had long ago started healing. It would never disappear.

Discarding his soiled clothing on the ground, he gathered her in his arms and carried her home.

A STRANGER

*T*he next morning was perfect, at first; then she had to remember the thousands of reasons why it wasn't.

There were no hypotheses now. She was a shifter. Zack was a Turner.

Shit, what was she going to say to her family?

"We'll tell them you've decided to move in here with your boyfriend."

Oh.

And there was that, too. The gorgeous, brooding male laying down next to her and playing with her hair. She had zero clue what to make of him. None. Hell, a week ago he didn't even *like* her. Now, they were- what…

"Bonded. Or mated, actually, I can't tell. I feel your worries so clearly – I wouldn't if this was an ordinary bond. Either way, you're mine."

He sounded way too smug about that. Shifting to look him in the eyes, she glared and added, "And *you're* mine."

"That goes hand in hand, beautiful. For the record, I always wanted you," he punctuated that with a quick kiss on her lips. "I just figured I'd better stay away; you weren't as durable back then. And I'm not exactly gentle."

He smirked, looking down at her naked body.

Hell. She was bruised all over. "That should be hurting like hell."

"Accelerate healing rate. One of the perks that comes with being one of us. Tell your cat she's one pretty beast."

It was all so weird; because she could *feel* someone – something – reacting to those words. The animal was… purring.

"I have a cat in my head."

"That somewhat oversimplifies it, but, for all intents and purposes, yes, you do." He cupped her head in his hand. "How are you feeling?"

Freaked out. Weird. Horny.

She settled on, "Good."

And strangely, she *was* feeling good.

"Awesome. Now, my phone's been blowing up for an hour, which means we're needed downstairs."

Instead of moving from the bed, he moved to top her, and pushed her legs apart with his.

"We're gonna have to make this round quick."

She laughed and curved her hips up as he entered her.

"I DON'T GET IT."

Hsu normally shared her vision with Rye or Ace first, but as the Alpha hadn't made any sense of it, they'd switched things up. She'd also shown what was to come to the rest of the pride.

The first part of the vision made perfect sense; there were people coming at them from all sides, surrounding Lakesides - but unable to cross the barriers Ace's witch friend had erected around the town to provide them with a layer of protection. Some people were coming for them - that much was clear.

Then, nothing. It was as if they hit a wall and bounced off it.

A wall made of mist.

Zack was as small and frail in that vision, just a little bigger than he was now, which means it would come to pass anytime soon; within days, weeks at most.

They were running out of time, and they needed answers.

As their problem was magical, and none of them could boast to know much about the ins and outs of witchcraft, Ace had called Rain.

It didn't bode well that the strongest witch they knew stared at them, as baffled as they had been.

"What, so you don't know how her visions could be blocked?"

"No, that part is easy. There are plenty of cloaking spells that could hinder Seers - but the thing is, if it was an easy spell, I should be able to break it. I pushed, and it didn't budge. And as I'm sure you don't want me to go hardcore on Hsu's mind…"

Daunte glared at her for even mentioning harming the kid.

"That's what I thought. I can't try anything else. *But,* what I don't get is the feel of that magic. I can tell you right now, it's not ancestral or elemental magic. Ancestral magic is based on words and spells. You'd hear whispers, chanting. Elemental - well, we'd feel if it was water, fire, wind, or earth; we'd smell it. This is something I've never encountered. And I'm going to be honest- I don't see any way around it. It hasn't only blocked the vision, it's possessed it. That red and black mist…"

"What did you say?"

The kids were normally excluded from this sort of conversation; no one wanted to worry them unnecessarily. But as Hsu was at the centre of the issue, Rye had told Niamh she could come in and observe. The two girls were inseparable, but it wasn't only that. Niamh was slowly getting more time during the adult meetings. Daunte hadn't asked why, but recalling the way she'd protected her adopted sister during their previous attack, he could guess. Rye saw potential in her; she'd make a decent Enforcer, one day, if she wanted to be.

"Nothing to worry about, sweetie, just because it's powerful doesn't mean that it's necessarily bad," Rain told the teenager, reassuringly.

But Niamh didn't look like she needed to be reassured at all. In fact, she seemed excited, and confident, too.

"Show me the mist," she asked Hsu.

"That might not be the best idea," Daunte stated, concerned about frightening her with visions of hundreds of enemies.

"I can handle it," the kid replied, rolling her eyes. "And, more to the point, I think I know what's blocking you."

That made everyone in the room more sceptical than hopeful; to their credit, she *was* thirteen.

"Sweetie…"

"No," Clari interrupted Rain, with a firm authority. She turned to Hsu, and smiled. "Show her." When Ace waggled an eyebrow at her, Clari just shrugged. "We've been talking about attacks for hours, anyway. I'm pretty sure that what Niamh's imagining is worse than reality. Besides, if there's a chance she can help, we need to listen to her."

Niamh looked like someone had just announced that they were pushing Christmas forward, and, after a second, Daunte smiled, pretty proud. Clari probably doubted her just as much as the rest of them, but she didn't let it show, treating Niamh like any other member of the pride.

The previous day, she'd suddenly become Beta of the pride because of their mating; most females who accessed the rank through bonding to a Beta, rather than fighting for it, were ill suited for it. Not his girl. She'd taken to it like a fish to water.

Hsu's hands went to Niamh's face, on either side of her forehead, and they remained perfectly immobile for a time.

Then, Niamh broke into a grin.

"That's what I thought," she said, straightening her spine.

She turned to the Alpha, and announced, "That red and black mist? I've seen it before. It's Tria's signature."

BETRAYAL

*T*ria. Clari immediately recognized the name, but no one else seemed to.

"The woman who saved you when you were ten?"

She'd only heard the story a few days ago, yet it felt like a century had passed since. Last Monday, she'd been human. Now, it was Saturday, and she was a feline shifter mated to the Beta of a small, yet powerful pride in danger.

Headtrip.

Niamh nodded.

"Yes. First time she appeared, there was a black and red mist - and she burst out from it, out of nowhere. I asked her about it, later, and she said it was how her power manifested itself. It was pretty cool, so I said I wanted to do the same thing, but she just laughed and said no one could. That it's *her* symbol. God knows I tried - but when I make mist, it's either gray, or the red is lighter, or darker. Basically, I can't copy *her* mark. Trust me, that was hers."

Niamh beamed when no one questioned her word.

"Doesn't she work for the Paranormal Investigation Agency?" Daunte asked, and the rest of the pride stiffened.

Clari felt compelled to take his hand and squeeze it, as some of his anxiety bled through to her. She could feel it in her bones, although she knew it didn't come from *her;* she didn't know enough to be suitably worried.

Her confusion must have hit *him,* because, he turned to her and explained, "The PIA is run by humans. If they hear about this, it means our secret is out. Our kind might want to kill you and Zack, but the PIA would probably make you test subjects."

"Right. Well, for the record, that was one of the instances where I would have felt better *not* knowing why you were freaking out."

He bumped her shoulder, and smiled. "No one is going to touch either of you. We just have to figure out how to survive. We always do."

Being bonded to him meant she could tell he wasn't feeling nearly as confident as he liked to appear, but she also saw that he had hope.

"Look, I know the PIA sucks, but we're not talking about *them*, we're talking about Tria. If *she* spoke for them, I'd be in a cell right now. Or dead."

Niamh got her phone out of her back pocket and held it up.

"So, we can just assume she's the enemy, and let her come against us without knowing what she's been sent for, or we can give her a call *now* and see if she's shielding us to *help us*. Remember, Hsu isn't the only Seer in the country."

Ace and Rye exchanged a glance, then Rye turned to Daunte, who nodded. Strangely - to her, in any case - they then looked at her. She tried not to feel too self-conscious as she also bobbed her head.

"So, let me get this straight, you want to take the advice of a thirteen-year-old and call someone who could potentially lead you all to your doom?" Rain asked, her tone perfectly even.

"That's about right."

She rolled her eyes and started furiously typing on her phone. "Better get Vivicia and Faith here, too. Wouldn't want to miss that party."

Niamh was practically skipping, and it was hard to ignore her unwavering faith in her friend, or her enthusiasm, for that matter. Plus, the fact that his mate clung to him, giving him all the support he didn't know he needed, helped through the worst situation they'd faced yet.

The Shifter Council wouldn't want to kill them all - although they would, if they had to - but they'd try their damnedest to get to Clari and Zack. The PIA was the opposite; and by far the worst of the two. They'd *want* to destroy the Wyvern pride, and the only member they'd care about saving would be his mate and his nephew, so they could be dissected and studied by their mad scientists.

Truth was, they didn't have a choice. Not really. If there was a chance - even a slim one - that the PIA may not end up being their enemy this time, they needed to take it.

"Wait," Daunte thought out loud, "What about avoiding the issue altogether? Can't we just prevent everyone from knowing what's happened? It's not like we socialize with other prides every other week. Maybe we can just…"

"It's too late," Rye replied, his ton curt.

Too late? They'd already been discovered? It made no sense. None. Clari had only just shifted a week ago.

Unless…

The very thought was poison to his mind, but he had to formulate it. Unless someone *inside* the pride had betrayed them. The temporary newcomers couldn't have - there was no way they'd connected the dots; they'd barely spent any time with them.

Daunte turned to his pridemates. Every adult was there, except Christine, Ola, Coveney and Tracy. Coveney was on patrol with the newcomers who'd applied as fighters, Tracy was upstairs with the kids, Christine, out on assignment. But Ola?

They never thought too hard about one of them being out for a few days. It was normal; they had a life, and their respective jobs sometimes demanded their presence elsewhere.

However, normally, he *knew* what the other members of the pride were up to. Ola…

He wasn't Alpha, but as Beta he still had the authority to search through the pride link. When he needed to. Closing his eyes, he concentrated as hard as he could, trying to find every member. He could feel them all - even Christine, faintly, despite the fact that she was out of town.

Everyone except Ola.

"She betrayed us."

He couldn't believe it, yet there was no other possibility.

"She did what she believed was just," Ace replied coldly. "And so did I."

She wouldn't say more in front of the kids, but taking in the glint in her eyes, he knew exactly what she meant. His sister had hunted her down the second she'd suspected the betrayal, and her body had been dumped in a ditch somewhere.

Good. Saved him the bother of doing it himself. He'd never hurt a girl, but he would have made an exception for her. Ola was kind and passionate, sweet, and fair. But she'd put his family and his pride at risk. There was no forgiving that. Not in their world.

"If she went to the Shifter Council, they may never stop hunting us. They might have relented, if they'd had nothing but rumors and suspicion; but a testimony from a member of the pride? They won't let this go."

ARRIVALS

*D*aunte remembered a time when he'd had a thing for Vivicia; now, he couldn't see it. She was pretty enough, he appreciated that – he even recognized what had drawn him to her to begin with: her spirit. But he was completely indifferent to it now. He'd been told that being mated or bonded dulled any feeling towards any other female, but he hadn't expected it to be so easy to ignore his old crush.

Plenty of bonded males still strayed on their females; Daunte knew he never would.

"You know, if you're gonna get in trouble twice a year, maybe we should just get to decorate one of your lake houses and call it a vacation home," Faith proposed, and Ace shrugged indifferently.

"Be my guest. But, guys, this is seriously going to get ugly. You may not want to…"

"Blah, blah. We'll stick around and help, if only because I know your mate is hiding an impressive wine collection he only pops open when you avert annihilation. So, should we talk strategy? You must have a plan."

Ace looked at Rye, who gestured her to go on.

"We think we can make them think they won. Create an illusion of sorts, making them believe Zack and Clari are dead. I have the body of a female at hand – that might help."

"Ooh! Who did you murder?"

"Our healer. She's the one who sold us out. So, if Rain could disguise her body…"

"Not a problem, but we still need a child. And regardless, that's short sighted. Yeah, they can believe they died, but then, what's step two?"

Daunte bit his lip, asking himself the same question. Only one answer came to mind.

"Then, we leave. Clari and I, with Zack. We take another name, and leave the continent. In a few years, once Zack is trained to control himself, we can come back to the pride."

He'd never seen his sister cry. Never. One single tear fell down her cheek as she nodded.

They had no other choice.

"There's also the matter of this... Tria. We need to know how she comes into play. Because she *does;* we can't afford to ignore what happens with Hsu's vision."

"She'll come," Clari said. "We've called, and as you said, the vision is clear. We'll get through this, you wait and see."

And wait, they did.

CLARI COULD DEAL with a change of domicile, a change of marital status, and a change of race all in the space of a week, but if they expected her to stay cooped up for one more second, god help her, she would add laxatives to all their coffees and escape while they were otherwise engaged. Or she'd find something equally evil if there weren't enough laxatives at hand.

The males, with Jas and Tracy, patrolled in turn, while Christine and Ace looked after the children. In the fortnight since she'd given birth, the Alpha had completely healed; the only reason why she didn't patrol was that they needed the most badass person available to stay around the kids. That was her.

Rye wasn't patrolling, either; he spent his time in his office, drawing lists of his allies, and discussing who they could call to their aid. With Ola's betrayal fresh in their minds, the list was short. It wasn't about finding people who were loyal to them; it was about trying to judge who would see past the fact that Zack was a Turner.

The first person they'd called was Ace and Daunte's parents; they were on their way to join them, no questions asked. Rye still hadn't called his, though, not quite sure about them, since the Royal Pride went against them in Hsu's vision. Niamh had also gotten in touch with the elusive Tria, but they hadn't received a response yet. The pride members tried their best to avoid showing it in front of the teenager, but that was the main cause of their anxiety. That woman was dangerous in every possible way - her connection to the PIA, and the way she interfered with Hsu's visions showed it. They needed to know where they stood with her; everyone wanted to believe that she would be on their side, but Niamh's word mattered less and less every day.

Meanwhile, as Beta, Daunte spent most of his time with the potential recruits, which majorly pissed Clari off, because her sole directive was to spend as little time as possible in their company. They weren't supposed to know about her yet; not until Rye included them in the pride, anyway. Given the fact that she'd either googled, or asked for clarifications on half of what they were talking about, she'd blow her cover in minutes if they'd hung out.

Still, it sucked. Because she, and her animal, wanted

time with her new mate, she was bored, grumpy, worried, and, finally, although she would never say it out loud, she *hated* the fact that one person amongst those recruits was a pretty, unmated female. A sensual brunette with bigger boobs than Clari's, rounder hips, and a petite figure she would have killed for. Ariadna, she was called.

Thinking the name was enough for her animal to want to push to the surface.

"You should let it out when it wants to be freed, you know."

Clari jumped up from the sofa where she'd been hosting her pity party, and turned towards the direction of the unfamiliar voice.

It was lower than any other female she knew, sounding husky, sensual, and when she saw the woman it had come from, she fit it to a T.

The stranger was perched on top of the kitchen countertop like she belonged there. She wore a tight, stretchy black fabric with a dozen pockets, and some hard, reinforced parts; it looked like a modern day armor. Wavy curls so dark they almost seemed blue were pulled in a messy bun on top of her head, staying clear of her sweetheart face, with a little turned up nose and a pouty mouth. She looked young, yet her dark eyes weren't. She looked relaxed, yet Clari's cat paced, wary.

"What are you doing here?"

The woman jumped down from the countertop with so much ease she may as well have been the cat shifter.

But she wasn't. Clari would have sworn she wasn't one of them - and certainly not a human being, either.

She tilted her head and smiled.

"I was called here," she replied in guise of explanation.

Clari stayed put. When she'd risen to her feet, she'd positioned herself between the woman and the entry-way; she wasn't moving. Past the entryway, she could go towards the stairs. Ace and the kids were in one of the recreational rooms on the first floor.

The stranger stared at her, assessing her, before chuckling.

"You definitely have a backbone," she told her. "Knowing I can kill you without breaking a sweat, and yet standing your ground. It's not something I see often. They should train you."

Clari froze as the woman advanced towards her. But, when she reached her, she just offered her hand.

"Demetria Winters. I go by Tria."

Her jaw practically hit the floor.

"You made me squirm on purpose."

She shrugged.

"Just a little. No better way to get to know people. You're the recently turned shifter."

That made her stop; had Niamh shared that already?

Catching her glance, Tria just smiled indulgently.

"Information is my currency of choice. I have my ways. Earlier, your cat wanted out. You want to give in when she does, especially at first. It makes the transition easier with time, and it also means she'll give in quicker, letting you shift back to your human form when you ask for it, rather than resisting. They should have told you that. Although, I'm sure your pride is currently occupied... Where's Niamh?"

The woman spoke at a thousand miles an hour, changing subjects so quickly Clari's head practically spun.

"Sorry," she grimaced. "I don't socialize much."

Suddenly, rather than noticing the fact that she was too perfect, moved too quietly, too fluidly, and had eyes that seemed to see right into her soul, Clari saw Tria and wondered if she was much older than her.

"Cool about the information; not cool that it's out there. Thanks for the tip about my cat. And yes, they're busy, but mostly, they don't really know what to tell me, because the shifter thing is *normal* to them. They never needed to adapt. As for Niamh- she's upstairs. I'd better call Ace and let her know you're here so you don't rip each other to shreds. She'll attack if you just turn up."

Tria shrugged indifferently.

"She'd try."

TRIA

*T*ria owned any room she entered without even trying, and the same could be said for Ace, so thrusting them in the same room was the equivalent of throwing a lightning bolt at a laser beam to see which one would explode first. After a staring contest that may have lasted until the end of time if Clari hadn't cleared her throat, the two females nodded, silently acknowledging each other's badass level.

After the proverbial game of *mine is bigger than yours,* Tria opened her arms, and Niamh jumped right in for a hug.

"I didn't think you'd gotten my message at first."

"I did. But I wagered you wouldn't contact me on my emergency line for a matter that could be sorted on

Skype, so I had to wait until I could get away unwatched."

"And did you?" Ace asked. "Get away unwatched?"

Tria rolled her eyes. "I'm going to try not to take that as an insult. Right, so, you have a Turner issue with one of these delightful little people," she said, waving towards the kids. "And everyone wants to kill you."

"Well, we know the Council and a pack who's wanted to get at us for a while are coming…"

"No, trust me. Everyone is on this, worldwide. You're the first things shifters agree on since they chose a full moon as a mascot in the dark ages."

Great. Just what they wanted to hear. It wasn't hundreds of shifters who wanted her and Zack dead; it was hundreds of thousands.

"But you can help, right?" Niamh asked, half frantic. "You can stop it. Hsu saw your mist; she saw your signature in her vision. That means you'll help us, right?"

How she clung to that hope; Clari would have loved to have that faith.

But, every passing day, she'd come closer to realizing and accepting the truth. Her restlessness, her frustration, her anger. She'd tried to displace it, but it was rooted in the fact that she knew her days were numbered. If all these people came to hurt her, she wouldn't let the entire pride suffer for her. She'd go meet them head on.

The issue was, they also wanted an innocent child.

Perhaps they could run, like Daunte had suggested. But where?

"Of course," Tria replied, matter of fact. "To every problem, there's a solution, and this one seems particularly simple."

Clari could see Ace hold Zack tighter, fully expecting Tria to attack. But the woman was still talking to her teenage friend, indifferent to the Alpha and the dozen pair of eyes on her.

But then she explained the details of her plan, and, for the first time in two weeks, Clari had hope.

CLARI HAD MET Daunte at the door with a radiant smile after his patrol, rather than the growingly sulking expression that he'd come back to over the last few days; but the real surprise awaited inside, sitting next to Niamh and waiting for him to explain her plan.

"How could that be possible?" Rye asked.

Tria smirked. "Leave it to me," she'd replied mysteriously.

"You're a Descendent, aren't you," Tracy blurted out from the other side of the room; she'd kept her distance from Tria, the magnificent creature who made everyone feel uncomfortable.

Rye and Daunte did their best to avoid looking at her, both hating the fact that they had to acknowledge just how breath-taking she was. The other males didn't mind.

"A Scion," Tracy added.

Daunte hadn't expected an actual response, but Tria just said, "Yes."

Well, this explained that. He was pretty certain he was allowed to find a goddamn modern-day goddess attractive. Although Clari would probably not see it that way if she even suspected he might like what he saw.

Then again, she'd salivated over Luke a time or two. That unpleasant memory alleviated any sense of guilt.

"Scion or not, we're talking about something I've never heard about before. Are you sure it's doable?" Rain asked.

"It won't be easy, and you'll still have to defend your-self *while* I take care of that. But yes, I can do it."

HERE THEY WERE AGAIN; waiting for their fate. This time, they did so without certainty, as Hsu was of no use whatsoever.

Tria had gone home.

"I need to go," she'd told a distressed Niamh. "Your little Seer saw enemies at your door; she saw you in this house the day it happened, remember? If I had been around, she wouldn't have seen *any* of that. Which means you would never have thought to call me."

Clari's head hurt trying to understand what she meant. "So, you're saying if you don't leave now, you'd change the future, which may change the past?"

Yeah, that made sense. Not.

"A lot of people think visions are a one-way street; but if you want them to come to pass, sometimes you have to work for them."

No one seemed to quite buy that.

"Right, let's try something. I'm staying," she announced. "I've one hundred percent decided to stick around."

Tria then turned to Hsu.

"See anything?"

The girl closed her eyes, and her mouth dropped open.

"It… changed. The vision. We're not in the lounge, we're outside. I still can't see but the block has changed. It's not just red anymore."

"Let me guess, some blue, some yellow, with a sprinkle of apocalypse on top?" then she turned back to Niamh. "I have to go. We have a plan that relies on the information we have at hand; in Hsu's vision, I wasn't around at the start of the battle, and *I came back* right after. That, we can deal with."

The Scion spoke softly to Niamh. While she seemed to look at all of them with something akin to indifference and contempt, there was real affection between her and the teenager.

She then turned to the Alpha.

"You need to contact me the moment your patrol spots them, and we know I don't come in until you're all standing in this lounge, in a circle. After that, we're flying blind. I *will* do my part, but in the meantime, it's up to you to survive this."

Just before she passed the threshold, Ace stopped her, calling, "Wait."

The two women had barely spoken to each other in the three hours Tria had stayed and everyone could feel the tension between them.

"You have no reason to help us. I want to trust you, but this…this is wagering our child's life."

Tria considered the words, before nodding.

"Yes, I understand how you may need some reassurance, given that everything is at stake for you, and I have nothing to gain in offering my aid. But three years ago, before you joined this pride, your mate took in Niamh. I do owe you a great deal for that. So, if it is of comfort to you, you have my word. When you call, I will come and I will do exactly what I said I would. I swear it on the River Styx."

On that note, she was gone.

Those last few parting words felt heavy, although Clari didn't understand why.

"I've heard that before; or read it in a book, maybe. That's a vow to the death; I mean, if *we* said it, it wouldn't matter at all, but in Greek mythology, nothing is as binding."

Ace turned to Niamh.

"You better tell me your friend is Greek."

THE END

*T*he tigress approached silently, but Daunte felt her; more importantly, he smelled her.

"Perfumed shower gel, really?"

Clari shifted back to her human form before cursing out loud.

"Dammit! Can't you just *tell me* what I'm not supposed to do, so I can surprise you once? Just the *once.*"

To his surprise, the day after Tria had left, she'd asked about potentially being trained.

"I need to be able to hold my own if there's a fight coming. No way am I sitting in the middle with the kids."

"That's *exactly* where you will be," he'd replied. But he had to relent on the second part. "However, I think we'll all breath much easier if you had some basic training under your belt. We'll start tomorrow."

If he was honest, Clari was a quick learner. Very quick. Her instinct was to let her animal take over during fights which meant she'd had no technique, but a lot of speed, strength, and dirty moves. Jas had given her technique on top of that.

But his mate hadn't wanted to stop there, fully intending to drive him insane. As soon as she could hold her own, she was asking, "I'd like to start patrolling with you guys."

Yeah… that was a no. Never. Not in a million years. Non-negotiable.

But when he'd said just that, she played dirty, and took sex off the table until he stopped being – her word – "unreasonable."

"Clari," he said, "they're coming for you. To *kill* you. So, no, you're not going to the front line. Especially not since you can't move quietly to save your life."

Hence why she was now attempting to prove that she could.

She'd gotten much, much better over the last week – but he wasn't going to relent on this.

"I'm supposed to be Beta female, and patrolling…"

"Is the Enforcer's job. I wouldn't be doing it if our pride wasn't so small, and if…"

He stopped talking, stopped breathing.

"What..."

Daunte lifted one finger to his mouth, gesturing her to keep quiet as he turned south, where he'd heard a noise.

He crouched, slowly, ready to shift and pounce. But a slight form came out of the shadows; a face he recognised, although he'd only seen it twice. Once on an application, another time, face to face.

The small blond Clari had pounced on the first time she'd shifted. Daunte never saw her again, which meant Rye had dismissed her...

If she'd made it to the pride house.

Was she spying on them?

He didn't think so; something made him believe she wasn't, although he couldn't place what.

"Five miles, on the other side of the river, there're bears on foot" she said. "More people are coming by road. They're close."

Then, the girl took a step back, returning to the shadow.

"Wait..." he called, needing a little more to go on; numbers, perhaps.

But he felt the change in the air that always preceded

a shift, and, a second later, a large bird of prey flew away.

Daunte didn't have the time to go after her. "Shift back, and stay close to me," he asked Clari, who for once, did as she was told. Thank all heavens for that.

They ran at high speed back to the pride house; Daunte burst into Rye's office in his animal form, the large panther making a mess of the files as he bumped into the furniture. He shifted, reaching for the closest phone.

"It's starting. Call everyone back."

CLARI HAD GENUINELY BELIEVED she'd been ready for it; that at the very least, she knew what to expect. What a load of bull crap.

She remembered all the things she'd told herself she'd do *later*. Call her mom to tell her about Daunte, see her aunt and uncle for dinner, visit her cousin, add apple muffins to the menu at the bakery they hadn't opened for nearly a month.

Now, if she messed up, there would be no tomorrow.

"Where is everyone?"

Her voice didn't relay even half of her panic, although it was shaky.

"They'll come. Jas and Ian are patrolling with the recruits. It's gonna be just fine."

How did Rye manage to sound so collected, damn it?

"It will," Daunte insisted. "That eagle girl gave us a huge advantage. We've been warned a good ten minutes earlier than planned. It'll be okay, beautiful."

Ace, who'd gone to call Niamh as soon as they'd arrived, came downstairs with all the kids, Zack held against her chest. She headed right to Clari, and put the sleeping child in her arms.

"Fitting to let this end exactly how it started," she said, attempting a smile.

"I can't…"

"You'll take care of him for me. And, if you need to, you just take the kids and run like hell. Run to the end of the world."

Clari couldn't speak, her throat dry and her heart about to explode, so she just nodded. She hated the very thought of it, but, if she needed to, she'd run; Zack and the other children deserved as much.

On that note, the Alpha left the house, Daunte, Rye, Faith and Vivicia on her heels.

Rain remained behind with her, chanting words in French, or perhaps Latin.

Then, she heard it as it started.

DAUNTE HAD NEVER LOVED his sister as much as he did when she made his mate stay behind. Because she would have died.

It looked like they all would.

Ace was the only one amongst them who hadn't shifted; in her human form, she was more powerful, as she managed to call to the beast within, using her fangs, her claws, and her raw power to dismember anyone who came close. Rye's curved canines punctured lungs and he clawed heads clean off. Daunte channeled everything his father ever taught him, becoming one with his beast, letting him loose on their enemy.

But wave after wave, they came at them, unrelenting. He heard the others around the house, although he couldn't see them. He felt them through the pride link. Some were wounded already.

Three minutes. They'd survived three minutes when the first one died.

Ace yelled out, her ferocity renewed as she felt their pridemate fade through the link.

She turned towards a cheetah to her right.

"You can go," she told him. "This is a damn massacre, you can just fucking go before…"

The cheetah jumped before her, his claws latching onto a bear's neck, and ripping it out.

There are children inside, Luke replied through the pride link, like nothing else mattered.

He shouldn't have been able to speak to them without being officially part of their pride, but the simple fact that he was there now changed that.

Although his attention was entirely engaged in the present moment, Daunte felt he wasn't the only addition. Ariadna, Sawyer, and Theo had also stayed.

He'd barely noticed them when another one faded away, Daunte couldn't tell which.

Four minutes, twenty-three seconds had passed.

They were all going to die.

Daunte had barely stopped a bear from slashing through his midsection when he saw another one charge from the corner of his eye. He didn't have a chance in hell to stop him.

At least his end would be quick.

THE ONE WORD TO describe his state of mind right now was confused. For a second, he wondered if he was dead and there *was* an afterlife, contrary to his beliefs. Then, he winced as just about every single muscle in his body hurt; opening his eyes, he saw a hand extended, offering him help standing up.

He took it gracefully.

"Thanks, man." Then, it had to be said, "Who the hell are you?"

The guy was cocky, dark haired, and a complete stranger. But Daunte was favorably inclined towards him given the fact that after his arrival, close to a hundred bear shifters lay dead in their garden.

"The name's Jason," the stranger replied. "We may have an acquaintance in common."

Then he lifted his head just as a flock of eagles darkened their view. "Pretty, socially awkward, too prompt to give a vow that may haunt her for all eternity."

Jason's eyes flashed, turning silver, and a colossal, unnatural lightning bolt tore through the sky.

"That would be my cousin Tria," he concluded, as three dozen birds fell on the ground, lifeless.

"Well, that was scary. And sexy." Ace thought it out, before amending, "Mostly sexy."

Rye lifted a brow, and she just shrugged. "What? It's not like I haven't seen you drool over Tria. They're weird and hot as fuck. Deal with it."

Daunte wasn't sure the man needed anything further feed his ego, but his previously cocky grin turned goofy.

"Thanks, lady."

"I can feel the rest of the pride is safe."

Those amongst them who hadn't died before the Scion's arrival, in any case.

"Did you get to them before coming to our aid?"

Jason's response was cut off by a sugary sweet voice coming from the other side of the house.

"That would have been me," a tall, pale blonde piped in, waving her hello. "Daphne," she introduced herself. "You owe me a pair of shoes. I'll never get the mud off the velvet."

THEY ALL STOOD IN A CIRCLE, surrounding the children, just like they had in Hsu's vision.

Well, not all of them. Clari didn't fail to notice two of them were missing. She didn't want to ask. She didn't need to either. She'd felt it in her bones. Sawyer and Tracy were gone. She didn't know the first one well, but Tracy- she couldn't wrap her head around it. Just last night, she'd said she'd finished her latest book. It would be her last, now.

Before she could wallow in that thought for too long, the doors opened in front of Tria. She'd come through for them – and, if she hadn't, Clari would have died. So would have Zack.

"It's done," she announced cheerfully, like she hadn't just accomplished something that defied the realm of possibilities.

Everyone breathed out, and Clari relaxed her posture. Daunte's arms wrapped around her waist and squeezed her hard.

HER PLAN HAD BEEN SIMPLE, and positively impossible, at least according to their witch, Rain, and every other member of the pride.

"The Council is coming; all twelve of them, conveniently in one place," she'd said. "And imagine if they all so happen to suddenly depend on the wellbeing of this little pride to survive. Well- you'll see just how quickly laws and decrees can be changed."

No one had understood what she'd meant at first.

"I can link their life force to Zack and Clari. If someone kills them, they'll all die, too."

"Impossible," Rain had replied, unable to wrap her head around it. "There's no spell that could accomplish that. Even if there *was*, if it went wrong-"

"It won't go wrong."

She'd been matter of fact.

And, apparently, she'd been right.

"WHERE ARE THEY?" Rye asked darkly.

"En route to their evil lair, I'm sure. And good thing, too, by the looks of it. If you'd killed them, they wouldn't be able to go home and change the laws, now, would they?"

"Do you really think they will?" Hsu asked.

Tria smiled at the child, before turning on her heels. "Why don't you see for yourself," she said, before walking out of door.

EPILOGUE

The Council was quick to act. Two days later, they'd made an announcement, and newspapers around the world were in danger of running out of ink over it.

Turners, they'd said, *were nothing more than legends until now.* A lie, and every shifter knew it. They'd existed all right; for a time. Then, the moment their nature was discovered, they'd been ruthlessly executed for the greater good. *But we have recently become aware that some very, very rare shifters are born with the ability to bestow the gift of an animal to human beings.*

These shifters are bound by very strict laws that will prevent them from exercising that gift without consent, and a careful vetting process.

They are a beautiful part of our heritage and will be protected at all costs.

Rye got the champagne out, and Ace drunk-texted Tria, to tell her she was a jerk for leaving so suddenly, without giving them the chance to thank her.

PS, she added, *we owe you everything.*

TRIA SMILED. She wasn't very good at dealing with thanks. Besides, it wasn't like she did everything to be nice.

There were three dozen groups of shifters, twenty-two powerful people, one witch, and an endless stream of loners who owed her. She liked it that way.

"You know, you can pretend that you're just a master-mind creating an army of servants, but you're not fooling us," Daphne told her- not for the first time. "You're acting that way because that's in your DNA. Your father's fatal flaw was also compassion."

"And your father's was hubris. You may be onto something, it *must* be genetic," she retorted, rolling her eyes.

"I don't get it, though," Jase butted in. "I mean, not the part about lending a hand to save the pretty kitten – that begs no question. The kid was cute. But that girl? Niamh? You've paid her a little too much attention."

"Don't you just *wish* you knew."

CLARI DIDN'T THINK she'd ever felt as awkward in her life. Ever.

"So, let me get this straight. One of his people *bit you* and made you into a, a…"

Marissa Thompson didn't finish her sentence, which may or may not have something to do with the fact that her sister had stepped on her toes. Hard.

"You must have been through a lot, dear," her aunt said, squeezing her hand in a sign of support. "I do wish you'd come to us about your problem." Then, she turned to Daunte, and sent him a smile. "But it sounds like your young man was wonderfully supportive."

"You're joking, right? You're supporting this farce? We should sue them. Set the PIA on them and…"

Train wreck. This was a train wreck.

She had no clue why Daunte had insisted on meeting her family. Or, rather, why he'd wanted her *mother* to be there.

Bethany and Andrew Turner had taken the news better than expected, but Marissa Thompson was… Marissa Thompson. Some people were cut to understand the whole parenting thing; others weren't. Marissa didn't have a supportive bone in her body – she never had, and never would.

"Please, feel free to attempt to do so," Daunte replied

pleasantly. "However, you may want to know that, firstly, the Agency is fully aware of the situation – secondly, I have the resources to outlast you in court twenty times over at the very least. And, if that's not enough, our pride *is* sitting on a few million. Above and beyond all that, our Alpha so happens to be royalty. You may want to rethink threatening me, or my mate."

Marissa narrowed her eyes, and added nothing, but Clari had to laugh, reading her easily, as she looked at Daunte more carefully now. She scrutinized the crisp suit he'd put on, the watch on his wrist, his posture. Daunte had made an effort today; he looked like a sexy, sexy businessman.

But what her mother saw was that he had money, and that was enough. She wouldn't have been nearly as vehement in her protests if she'd known that from the start.

"We're not here to fight," he said, ignoring Marissa, and looking directly at her aunt and uncle. "In fact, we're not here for you, at all."

Clari frowned, confused when he got up from his seat. Then, she started hyperventilating. Daunte bent a knee, and got a small black box out of his pocket.

"We're here for you, Clarissa. You were thrown into our world and you never even tried to escape from it. You've accepted every single bit of crap coming along with it, fangs, fur, and all. We're here because you deserve everything you've ever wanted. You're my mate, and, in my world, that's everything. Let me become everything in yours."

The End.

Next in the series: Catnip.

NEXT IN AGE OF NIGHT...

The entire pride know that they wouldn't have made it without help; the Scions were a humongous part of it, but without an early warning, giving them ten precious minutes, who knows how many of them would have died?

Meet Ava in Catnip, Coveney's story.

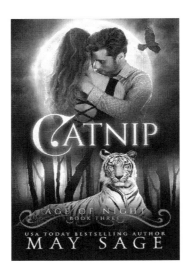

NOTE THAT TRIA, Daphne and Jason's books won't be published in the Age of Night series.

Stay in tune for a short excerpt of their world.

REALM OF DARKNESS

EXCERPT (UNEDITED AND SUBJECT TO CHANGE)

*T*he basement where they were tucked away wasn't anyone's idea of a prison; for one, there was no lock on the door, and it also contained everything a bunch of twenty-somethings might have wanted. Flat screen, books, computers, and a gym amongst other things.

The gym area was where they stood today. Tria, Daphne and Jase were perfectly still and silent, each one of them at one end of the triangle drawn on the training floor. Then, all of a sudden, although no one had given a signal, they all moved.

An outsider looking in would have assumed that they were trying to kill each other. Jase used every inch of his hulking figure to launch himself at Daphne, who evaded him just in time, drop kicking his head as she was at it. Tria was the vicious one; she let them exert themselves before attacking both, jumping in the air and kneeing Daphne right on the chest, before flipping towards Jase. He was waiting for her, holding a man-size punching bag he threw at her.

In fact, they were just letting off some steam. The last few days had been stressful for them. As discussing the matter troubling their minds hadn't helped, they'd opted to work some frustration out of their system instead.

They'd started without warning, and they stopped as quickly. One second, they were seemingly attempting to tear each others apart, and the next, they sat calmly, not a hair out of place, their breathing controlled, their stance relaxed.

An instant later, their door opened in front of three outsiders.

TRIA WASN'T prone to gawking. She'd seen too much in her lifetime to be surprised or impressed by much; yet, she gawked then. So judge her. The guy was hot.

His dirty blond hair was a little long on top, and cropped short on the side; there was the outline of a tattoo running from his neck and plunging under the tight, dark compression shirt that hugged his define torso. Lucky shirt. She saw some ink peeking from his sleeves, suggesting that the design was extensive. He wore a combat uniform, and reeked of the unbearably cocky attitude most field agents sported. Normally,

Tria rolled her eyes; today, she was practically certain there was a bit of drool at the corner of her mouth. Not that it mattered. No one saw her mouth under the mask she generally wore at work.

Two other men were walking a few steps ahead of the stranger, and while her attention was mainly focused on the hottie, Tria saw them. Of course she did; her mind never shut down enough to stop assessing threats.

The stranger was also in his fighting uniform. He stood a little shorter, slightly bulkier than the hottie, with darker hair and a serious expression. To actually be fair in her observation, she had to admit that they both belonged on the cover of a fashion magazine, but Tria didn't feel any pull towards that one.

The older man leading the small party was the only full fledged human in the room, and it showed. His imposing frame and intense dark eyes would have commandeered attention in any other company, but here, the only real power he possessed was strapped to his jacket - a badge saying Andrew M. Crawford, Director.

Andrew's gaze swept the "office" where her team worked; Daphne hunched over her computer, frantically typing, while Jason played video games. None of them were actually working, and the presence of the man who was technically their boss didn't phase them.

"Tria," the Director called out, when he saw her

perched on her favorite spot: the window at the far corner of the floor. There was relief in his tone when he found her there, and it made her narrow her eyes. He needed her - which was never a good thing.

She jumped down and walked to the Director, doing her very best to avoid looking at the hunk behind hm, and only failing three times.

She never liked meeting new people in the Agency. They looked at her with obvious disdain, because of her appearance. Most Agents ranged in various degrees of weird, but no one else wore a medical mask to cover the lower part of their face, and a pair of glasses so large and dark they could basically be qualified as a ski max.

"Tria, meet Grayson Parker, and Ralf Daniels, the best field agents we have."

Ralf hid a grin, but Grayson didn't seemed phased by the praise, rolling his eyes.

"Gray, this is Tria Winters. She leads this team - they know more about the paranormal world than all of us combined."

Gray's brow rose by an inch; he was visibly doubtful about that last statement, but all he did was extend his hand. So did Ralf, and she purposefully shook his, first.

She had to give them that; neither of them acted like

they believed she was a freak. That could only mean one thing: they were used to weirder.

When she moved her hand to return the hottie's greeting, he lifted it, and dropped his lip on the back of her palm, smirking against her skin. Tria didn't say, or do anything, because the instant their skin touched, her entire body froze.

What the ever fucking hell was *that*? Her mind raced through thousands of possibilities, and settled on incubus. The man had to be an incubus to get that reaction out of her.

He was also a prick who knew *exactly* what he was doing.

Glaring behind her glasses, she pulled her hand back, and cleared her throat. Eventually, she remembered how the whole speaking thing was supposed to work.

"To what do I owe the pleasure?"

Andy started to speak, but Gray was not on to stand in the background; he cut off his boss, explaining, "I had a simple mission this morning, and it went wrong. I was stung with demon venom."

She didn't think anyone had ever said that in such a blasé, dismissive tone, just as if he'd been discussing the weather. Most people would be too busy whirling in pain on the floor to have a chat. Tria reluctantly attributed him a couple of badass points for that.

"Where's the wound?"

She shouldn't have asked. The guy shot her a dazzling smile before removing his compression shirt unceremoniously, revealing a lean, but absolutely ripped upper body. Yep. She was really drooling now. Praised be the mask.

The only problem was that the man knew just how pretty he was.

Cocky isn't your thing, Winters, she admonished herself as he turned, revealing large shoulders, taut muscles sculpted on his frame. There was a bandage around his left shoulder, and she concentrated on that.

"I'm going to have to take a look."

Gray turned his head towards her, and said softly, "Be gentle with me, ma'am."

Tria shook her head, speechless.

"Does he ever stop laying on the charm?" she asked Andy, out of curiosity.

The Director seemed to think it through, but Ralf's reply was immediate and final. "*Never.*"

Slowly, carefully, she peeled it back to look underneath.

The wound wasn't pretty, red and green, blotched and grained, betraying the demonic origin. It was healing though, and quickly, if he'd only been stabbed in the morning.

"It's pretty deep too," she remarked, to no one in particular. "What kind of demon?"

"One with tentacles," Ralf replied, moving his fingers to imitate the creature's Whirling. Gray winced at the memory. "plus a few different heads."

"Sounds messy."

"I generally like messy."

She pulled the bandages back in place, and took a step back. She took a long relieved breathe when she was out of his personal space. Damn him, but that man smelled way too good. Way, way, too good - which did support her theory that he might have been an incubus.

Not that it mattered. Ninety five percent of the staff of the Paranormal Investigation Agency was, well, paranormal. The Agency employed vampires, wolves, djinns, nymphs, and everything in between. Humans were practically powerless against paranormals, so it made sense to fight fire with fire.

"Looks like an Asmoderian's claw. The usual antidotes should work out - I'm sure whoever took care of you gave you one. The only difference is, while the venom works its way out of your body, you'll probably act a little rash. Give in to your instincts rather than questioning them."

Gray and Ralf exchanged a glance that told her everything.

"You've already started acting rash," she guessed. "That's why you're here."

"I may or may not have tied the human who summoned these freak to a chair, and locked him in with a hellhound. In my defense, it was a perfectly well trained hound - and the guy needed a wake up call."

Tria concentrated on the most important piece of information here. "You have a trained hellhound?"

Gray gave her his very first real smile - not the charming crap he liked to dish out, and he nodded. And, another five badass points for the hunk.

"The point is, this was completely out of character. He insist that he's fit for work - I'd like you to confirm that."

The answer was, no, he wasn't fit for work; not even a little bit. He was going to tie more idiots to chairs, and possibly put a dildo up Andy's ass, if he stepped out of line.

Tria smirked.

"Sure. He'll be just fine," she lied.

The two agents stared at her, speechless, and suspicious.

"Really? Because he has another two missions out with civilians, and we can't risk…"

Tria rarely looked at anyone in the eyes; right then, she did, meeting the Director's gaze. "I'm sure. Talking about slightly imbalanced agents in public, I put a request through last month. I don't think we've had an answer yet."

Andy tensed, with good reasons.

Tria had asked for her team to get out of the compound; not on an assignment, but for a night of fun.

"Come on, Andy. Nothing has happened these last five years." Another lie. "It'll be good for the moral."

A bead of sweat ran on the Director's forehead. He'd looked right at her for too long, now.

"Alright. You can go this weekend. But you have to keep them in check, Tria."

She smiled underneath her mask, before turning her heels, heading back to her window, wordlessly dismissing them.

Andy, and the rest of the high ranking officials in the Agency often forgot one simple fact.

Grayson - venom-bit or otherwise - and other agents like him, weren't their worst problem. Nor were human-summoning demons, and pathetic fiends roaming the cities, living for their next mischief.

She was.

She, and the rest of her team.

Just before they walked out, Gray turned and mouthed a silent *thank you.* She shrugged it off. She hadn't lied to help him; she'd lied because she didn't give a damn what he did to the Agency.

"That was two incredibly hot asses," Daphne said, the moment the door had closed.

"Would you stop objectifying my sex for one goddamn second?" Jase growled, without taking his eyes off the screen, shooting zombies.

"Hmm." The woman pretended to consider it. "Nope, I don't think I will. Have you seen their biceps?"

Had she *ever.*

"Now this delightful distraction is out of the way, we can either go back to kicking each other's asses, or finish discussing our issue. The Heir wants our answer, and I got the feeling he isn't the patient type."

Tria sighed. They'd talked about it all week, and today, they'd sworn to come to an agreement. That was how they worked: together. Their parents had made the mistake to go against each other and everyone knew how *that* had ended. That didn't mean they always agreed.

Daphne was all for joining the Heir. Jason was vehemently against it. Tria…

"Everything he says makes sense. The Agency has

either controlled, enslaved or incarcerated people like us for the last five years, and it needs to end. *But* I don't trust that person. I don't trust his motives. And I sure as fuck don't intend to swear my allegiance to anyone. Anyone but *us*."

As far as the agency was concerned, she was the leader of the Omega team, mainly because she was the only one with enough patience to play nice with their authority. In actual fact, they were the corner of a triangle - each equal to the next, working in perfect balance. Her word didn't have more weight than Daphne's or Jason's.

But as she happened to be right, her cousins nodded.

They would bow to no one.

THE INFERNAL THREE will include books twice as long as my usual novels and novellas.

It's available on preorder on all retailers.

EXCERPT OF CATNIP

UNEDITED

*C*oveney's animal jumped out of the way, blocking the attack of the Vergas wolf with ease, and buried his sharp fangs in his flanks. A pained growl was ripped from his chest and he turned to see an arrow lodged in his shoulder.

Shit. His tiger wouldn't be able to get rid of it, and shifting back to his human form in the middle of this mess was nothing short of suicidal. He'd only taken a second to contemplate how screwed he was when another wolf jumped him from the right; he saw another set of arrows aiming at him on the left.

Arrows…

He knew someone who used those, and she rarely missed her mark.

You're screwed, he told himself. He was - there was a

179

chance that they all were. But inside their home, there was nine children, two of whom would die if he failed.

Zack, his Alphas' newborn, was condemned by shifter laws because of what he was: a Turner, able to change a regular human being into one of them. Their existence was a secret shifters had spilled a lot of blood to keep under check. Lola, their toddler, wouldn't live much longer. The Vergas wolves had wanted to kill her, hunting him everywhere, until his Pride had managed to push back. But today, if things went their way, they'd have a chance.

Unless he stood his ground as long as possible to give the children a chance to run, with their Beta female. He had to survive.

Launching himself as the wolf, Coveney's cat roared as a second arrow pierced his skin, closer to his heart this time.

It wasn't the first time he'd been shot. It hurt like a bitch but he could ignore the pain. He had to.

His claws ripped through the wolf's back; he placed a paw on its head and, with a flicker of his wrist, broke his neck. Then, he turned left, and there she was. Smirking. Of course she smirked. She was finally getting what she'd wanted for the best part of a decade.

LORREN HADN'T WAYS BEEN that way. Back in the

days, she'd actually been a sweet kid; his very best friend. He couldn't even pinpoint when things had started to change, exactly, but he remembered when he'd realized there was no going back, not for them.

Coveney noticed women had tits late for a shifter; he was nineteen when he found as girl that fascinated him more than a video game. Lorren disliked Holly on sight, but Coveney figured it was just the usual best friend vs girlfriend thing. Until the day he'd been called to his Alpha's office, accused of rape.

With some distance, he now saw he'd been a dumb fool. Lorren had been into him; she'd probably seen them as a thing, because there had been no other woman in his life. Not that it justified the way she'd ruined his life.

Almost everyone turned from him, believing her words over his. Holly, his family, his friends. There were a few notable exception; the Prince who left his family Pride, going with him, rather than letting him become a loner. Those who followed.

The Wyvern Pride. They were everything to him. No wonder Lorren smirked as it was burning to the ground.

Lorren got entangled in another lie, years after his departure, and the Royal Pride ordered a witch to cast a truth spell, this time. His name was cleared in the process. Her punishment was becoming a Squire, a slave of the Royal Pride, which explained what she was doing here. There was no doubt that she hated his guts now more than ever.

Coveney saw a dozen of familiar faces behind her. He was relieved to see his own family, and his Alphas, was notably absent. The Royal Pride hadn't sent its official after them - these were just a bunch of stuck up idiots who'd acted on their own.

He could see Lorren's glee from a distance as she shot arrows after arrows - all in his direction. He had to deflect adversary on a one on one *and* avoid getting shot again.

Coveney's tiger screamed out again as a wolf head punched his right in the shoulder where he'd been shot. Falling to his side, he saw another arrow fly, aiming right to his heart now he was knocked over.

He almost closed his eyes.

A split second before the weapon found its mark, a high pitch scream resounded in the skies.

Great. Eagles. The servant of the shifter council had joined the party. Not only was he going to die - he was dying, knowing his Pride was doomed.

That was his last thought when the magnificent bird of pray descended, plunging at high speed towards the driveway-slash-battlefield.

And caught the arrow in its talons, before batting its large wings and flying back up.

HUNKY BEAST

WONDERING WHAT HAPPENED TO
THE GIRL DAUNTE SAVED?

*H*er lungs were going to explode, her limbs begged for mercy - her treacherous mind whispered that a short break, just thirty seconds to catch her breath, couldn't hurt. She knew better than to listen to it.

She already had zero chance of making it out of the forest. This was a last desperate attempt to grasp at her freedom, but she was running from the worse kind of predators, and they *would* catch her.

They always did.

Emily came to a sudden halt when a SUV entered her field of vision, its driver honking as hard as he could. Shit. It was heading right at her, headlight blinding her. She cursed as she did her best to run for cover. Who drove in the middle of a damn forest at dawn anyway? Her heart beat fast as she guessed the answer.

Them. It had to be one of them.

Her panic only lasted an instant; the car managed to avoid hitting her, swerving just in time, and then, the driver popped his head out of his window. Emily breathed in relief, because he definitely didn't belong to the pack she was running from. She knew them all - their face, their voices, their stench. She doubted she'd ever forget them.

"What the hell are you…" he started, but he stopped short after getting a good look at her.

She'd definitely seen better days.

Emily was wearing a dirty pair of short and her blouse had been white once; now, under layers of swear, dirt and blood, it most definitely wasn't. She didn't have any shoes on, and her left ankle bore a angry wound - it had spent the last few weeks bound to a bed frame.

The stranger tone's changed, and his anger was replaced by worry. "Are you alright?" he asked, pinning her under his intense gaze.

In other circumstances, she might have reacted very differently - this was incontestably the most handsome man she'd ever met. As things were, she noticed, but couldn't have cared less. He could have been a hundred years old, have warts, claws, and a hunched back for all she cared. She was pretty certain she was done with men for the rest of her days, after her experience.

Emily bit her lip, considering her answer. She probably shouldn't involve that poor guy, but what choice did she have?

She did the only thing she could: telling the truth.

"No. I was abducted. I need to get away from here, fast."

The stranger nodded, and gestured her towards the passenger door of his car.

"To the police?" he offered, returning to his driver sea,t but she shook her head. She didn't have the time for that, and *they* might very well wait for her there. It wasn't like the human authorities could protect her in any case.

No one could.

Her best hope was using every single resources she had to try to disappear.

She'd try to run four times, but she'd never managed to make it out of the forest; as the truck past the wooden borders at high speed, she felt everything inside her tense. This was really it. Her one chance.

Her savior's voice pulled her from her reveries when he said, "Ah. Shifter problem."

Her head shot to him, as she wondered how he'd guessed. It wasn't like shifters were the only criminals out there - there were demons, vampires, angels, and even plain old human who targeted the weak for kicks.

Weak. She'd never thought she was amongst those, but life had shown her just how wrong she was.

"Have you done this before?" the guy asked her.

She wasn't sure what he meant, but she shook her head. None of this craziness was familiar to her. A few months back, she'd been nothing but a normal woman - an accountant, for Heaven's sake. Then, her entire world had crashed and burned after one phone call.

The driver turned to her and sniffed the air.

"I smell fur on you. Wolf. There's something else underneath. Something wilder...is it water?"

Fuck. So that's how he knew. And there was a very good chance that, to be able to tell, he was one of them - another shifter. She may very well have jumped right out of the pan, and into the damn fire.

The man didn't pause long enough to give her the chance to answer.

"You'll want to lay a false trail. Don't contact anyone you're familiar with, and never use anything that could lead them to you - phone, credit card. Don't go anywhere predictable; nowhere you've seen before, not even a place that you've told your best friend you wanted to visit. Take various transports to get there, too. Wolves are the best trackers; they'll find you if you let them."

He sounded calm, almost matter of fact. With a secretive smile, he answered the question she didn't ask, "My pride has ran from wolves a time or two."

Pride. That was what feline shifters called their packs; Emily hadn't remembered that from what she'd read online.

"You're a cat."

The man flashed her a dashing smile, his eyes blazing gold before returning to amber.

"Panther. And it's not exactly polite to ask, *siren.*"

A chill ran through her bones. He knew. The wolves who'd kidnapped her had spent months observing her, checking all the facts before being sure, but after a two minutes car journey, he just knew what she was.

"Don't fret. It's not written on your forehead; I've just met one of you before. You give off the same vibe."

Their conversation had been pretty one sided until then, but that made her open her mouth.

"They said…" she croaked, her throat so dry she didn't recognized her own voice. "The guys who were holding me said my kind was supposed to be extinct. That I'm the only one."

The stranger chuckled low. "Here's some news, puppet. Psychotic kidnappers tend to lie."

He might have a point.

"I'm Daunte Cross, by the way."

Coming soon.
Follow me on Facebook for news! <3

Printed in Great Britain
by Amazon